Shattered

Memories

C W Clarke

Shattered Memories

This book is a work of fiction. Names, characters, events and places are all used fictitiously or are a product of the author's imagination.

Copyright © 2021CWClarke

All rights reserved.

ACKNOWLEDGMENTS

I would like to say a big thank you to everyone who read my early attempts and encouraged me along the way, your support and feedback is very much appreciated, I won't list you all but you know who you are, I couldn't have done this without you.

Chapter 1 Lucy

It was always the same house; the bricks are a warm rusty red set against the deep green of the Georgian window frames. The house stands tall and proud, it dominates the eerie landscape. The welcome feeling of the summer sun is melting my body while the sweet scent of summer flowers fill the air. Then suddenly the familiar feelings of panic are flooding through my body at speed, invading my mind and clouding my senses. I wake up with a gasp, my limbs are a tangled web in the bed covers, and my heart is pounding a frantic rhythm as the sweat rushes from my pores taking with it some of the fear. I'm gasping for air but I can't breathe, with every attempt my lungs make to draw breath the air around me becomes thick and heavy as it slips ever further out of reach.

Sometimes it feels as though I am watching the world from above, mine is a life being lived that belongs to someone else. I'm watching without having any control, I feel like I am a spectator in the shadows of my own life. My breath finally comes to me in short ragged gasps but then within seconds the air has gone again. My body is trembling uncontrollably and all I can feel is a deep aching pain and a terrible loss.

I've managed to drag myself up so that I'm sitting on the edge of the bed, my knuckles are turning white because I'm holding on too tight to the duvet that I am nervously bunching up in my fists. My eyes are frozen wide open with fear, as my breathing begins to slow the world releases its suffocating hold on me. Slowly the fog in my head clears and my vision settles, I take in the welcoming sight of my bedroom. I am putting all of my effort into breathing slowly as I've been taught to do, my heart rate slows and I'm hit with the realisation that it's just a dream. A dream that feels inescapably real but intensely familiar. It is utterly terrifying.

These dreams have been haunting me for years now, although to call them dreams doesn't seem a strong enough word to convey the terror they evoke in me each and every time they decide to strike. Over the years, Chris, my husband, has tried numerous times to persuade me to get professional help to deal with my nightmares, but each time he brings it up I refuse, because as strange as it seems I don't want the dreams to stop, they feel far too real to simply erase, they are a part of who I am. I feel like they are telling me something, or maybe they are warning me of something that is yet to come, maybe of a tragedy that is waiting to strike. Chris doesn't understand how I feel so it's got to the point now where I've stopped telling him about them when they happen. I've had professional help in the past to deal with the panic attacks so at least I know what to do when my body is taken over by the fear. Chris has missed most of my more recent episodes because he sleeps through anything, his ability to sleep so deeply despite wailing children or thunderstorms usually frustrates me but now it means I have an easy secret to keep.

Dawn is fast approaching now and although I'm tired deep down into my bones I give up on any hope that sleep will claim me again. There's too much to do today so I decide to make an early start. As deeply as I love my two children the few hours early in the morning before they are both awake is precious time not to be wasted. I wrap up in my old dressing gown and pull on a pair of fluffy socks before going downstairs in search of Lupo the dog and some coffee.

I pause briefly and glance at the mirror that hangs at the bottom of our stairs, the woman looking back at me looks like an older version of what I should look like, I am thirty-two but the reflection before me belongs to a much older woman. My blue eyes appear to have lost their sparkle and they are rimmed by dark purple circles, my blonde hair hangs dull and limp to my shoulders, I lean forward and turn my head to the side, then I roll my eyes to catch a glimpse of my profile, I look like a ghost.

As predicted, our golden retriever Lupo wakes up as soon as he hears me enter the kitchen, just like he has done every other morning for the last six years, he had been found abandoned in a supermarket car park in early February, he was thought to be a Christmas present that was no longer wanted. Chris and I rescued him from a life of living in the animal shelter and he quickly became a part of our family. He lifts an eyelid and shakes the sleep from his head, his tail thumping in his basket as he does so. His normal morning routine is a quick run around the garden to chase away any squirrels who have dared to enter while he was sleeping, I meanwhile start on a pot of coffee while I wait to let him back in.

I stand by the window and watch Lupo sniffing the base of his favourite tree, a blackbird startles him then he races around a few laps of the garden before looking at me through the glass door to be let back in. Once he's back inside we sit in companionable silence at the kitchen table with his head resting against my leg, I find his weight against me both soothing and comforting.

My parents are arriving this afternoon for the Christmas holidays so I want everything to be ready for their arrival, it's been a long busy term that only ended yesterday. Tomorrow is Christmas Eve so my plan is to complete as much as possible today so I can relax and enjoy this time with my family. Chris and I are both only children and his parents are having Christmas in Mexico this year so it will be a quiet time for us here. I found it odd that his parents have had all year to go away but waited until Christmas time to go but they assure me December is the best time to visit Mexico. Chris has never been very close to his parents and they always seem a bit distant with their grandchildren so it's not too disappointing. He told me early on in our relationship that he knew he had been an accident, his parents both had career plans to follow and a baby did not feature anywhere in their plans, they didn't intend to alter their lifestyle to accommodate him either.

He went to boarding school from a young age and only saw his parents during the holidays, then as he got older he spent holidays with friends, either at their houses or enjoying holidays in exotic locations, the cost was never an issue with his parents, they were happy to write cheques if it meant he was off their hands. Chris says he was happy enough without having his parents featuring too heavily in his life. They are always polite when I see them which admittedly isn't very often, and when they've spent time with Jasmine and Harrison they've proven that they really don't know how to act around children, they talk to them as though they are adults, they try to talk about the news or their next holiday, nothing that any young child would know how to reply too. They send each of them a large cheque for birthdays and Christmas and that's as much involvement as they seem to want. I put their money straight into the bank so the children can buy a car or something else useful when they are grown up.

I finish my to-do list which is thankfully much shorter than I had anticipated, my mum and dad don't expect anything fancy while they are here, they are just coming to relax and spend time with us, and they are very easily pleased. As long as there isn't a shortage of teabags or mince pies they will be content playing the endless stream of board games Jasmine and Harrison have got planned for them.

Mum and dad moved up to the Norfolk coast when they retired a few years ago, up until then they lived nearby, here in the same sleepy Suffolk town, I'd never felt the need to move anywhere else because I was always happy here. It was initially hard when they moved away but they had always dreamed of living by the water. Dad bought a little boat that he spends hour upon hour tinkering with while my mum cooks cakes, reads crime fiction, and potters around their garden, she has even started growing her own vegetables. It's a shame I don't see them as much as I used to but it's great to see they are enjoying their retirement and their time together after years of working hard and taking care of me. They truly love being grandparents and jump to any opportunity to spend time with their grandchildren.

All that remains to do today is to give the spare room a quick clean so it's ready for them, I did it last weekend but then when I hid in there to wrap the children's presents a few nights later there was an explosion of glitter from the roll of wrapping paper. Then I need to make another batch of mince pies because the last batch that I made disappeared within twenty-four hours. The grocery delivery is due to arrive this morning leaving me time to run to the shops this afternoon if anything vital has been forgotten. I'm feeling quietly relaxed now and looking forward to the festivities. I've always loved Christmas but now that I have my own children it feels like an extra special time of the year, I understand what people mean when they talk about the magic of Christmas.

I make myself another coffee and go through to the conservatory that leads off the kitchen, a recent addition to the house but one I had wanted ever since we moved in almost seven years ago after our wedding. We only just managed to afford this house, money was tight but after my mum and dad gave us a very generous cheque as our wedding present it was made possible, they had been saving for years ready for when the day came that I wanted to own my first home. Chris and I had always rented previously but we knew we wanted a family home ready for when the time came for having our children.

Something about this house made me fall in love with it at first sight. Chris wasn't quite as keen to begin with but I could see beyond the peeling paint of the exterior and the crazy choices of paint colours inside, so after a few viewings he agreed to take on the mammoth task of renovating our home, which was aptly named Hope Cottage.

It took us almost six months of cleaning and painting well into the evenings, or sometimes the early hours of the next morning. Slowly the rooms came back to life as we ripped up the old musty carpets unearthing several small armies of spiders in every room, we sanded and painted the floorboards, ripped out the rusty old plumbing in the bathrooms and kitchen and replaced it with new pipes and gleaming white appliances. The walls seemed to double in size when we painted them a bright fresh apple white and the light flooded in. You could almost hear the rooms breathing again as the house slowly became our home.

We didn't have a social life at all during that time, if we saw friends they were bringing us takeaway food and painting alongside us. I was still working full time teaching high school science and Chris was up and gone at the crack of dawn each day into the office, he left early so he could be home as early as possible to climb the ladders and paint ceilings, or lay new skirting boards or take on whatever challenge awaited him next. It was an exhausting time but also a time of happiness and excitement, we couldn't wait to fill our home with a family. The dreams haunted me less frequently during that period of time, maybe because I fell into an exhausted heap as I crawled into bed each night. I barely had the energy to dream, although sometimes, when I least expected it I would have a sudden flashback of an image from one of the dreams, I would see the face looking back at me in the reflection of a window, or just catch a glimpse of it as I closed my eyes last thing at night.

My eyes are drawn to the view outside in my garden where the frost is blanketing the grass, it is creeping upwards and wrapping the trees in a furry white cover, strings of fairy lights are woven between the branches where they are twinkling, dancing hauntingly in the wind. My mind returns to my dream and I find my breathing quickens as the feeling of panic rushes back to me, I can see his face clearer than ever before, I'm looking deep into his eyes. I can hear the piercing screams tearing through the silence.

Several minutes pass and yet I still feel unsettled, then because it is still quite early I tiptoe back upstairs almost holding my breath. I'm being as quiet as can, trying not to wake anyone. I feel chilled deep into my bones as I slip back into bed beside Chris, I'm trying but failing to absorb his warmth. I feel my breathing beginning to steady but my thoughts are racing, the face is so clear in my mind but who is he? Who is that little boy? Is he real or just a figment of my imagination?

The next thing I know is that I'm being crushed, by two highly energetic children who have woken up and decided it is breakfast time, I glance at the clock and realise they are right. I can't actually believe I went back to sleep for almost an hour. Jasmine and Harrison are looking gorgeous in their Christmas pyjamas and as they snuggle up to me it helps to erase some of the feelings from earlier this morning. Chris still looks exhausted as he rolls himself over in an attempt to wake up so I offer to make the children some cinnamon pancakes for breakfast, they have a few jumps on the bed and then they run down after me leaving Chris to have another few precious minutes of sleep.

Once Jasmine came along I stopped working altogether, then just as I was thinking it was time to go back to work I discovered I was pregnant again with Harrison. When he was a year old I went back to teaching three days a week. It's a big help financially but Chris still works crazy hours to make up for the two days that I am at home. He works with data software doing something I have never pretended to understand, it pays well and he gets to work from home for a day most weeks which means he gets to attend school shows, sports days, and other events that the children might have.

The cinnamon pancakes are a great success, Jasmine and Harrison have eaten three each and washed them down with a mug of warm milk, the pancakes even manage to lure Chris from his duvet cocoon, he stumbles into the kitchen still wrapped in the duvet and rubbing the sleep from his eyes, however, the combination of strong coffee and a stack of pancakes soon revives him. Once he has finished his breakfast he decides to walk Lupo and he takes the children with him too, meanwhile, I tidy up ready for my parent's arrival later on.

It doesn't take long to tidy up once I'm alone with just the radio for company, by the time Chris and the children come back having stopped at the cafe in the park for a hot chocolate with special Christmas shaped marshmallows the house is looking its best. The groceries are all put away and the smell of cinnamon still clings to the air evoking a Christmassy smell. I am feeling peaceful and content.

The children have both decorated some of the gingerbread men that we made yesterday, and they've helped to make a selection of sandwiches and cakes, so that at Jasmines suggestion we can have a

Christmas themed picnic for lunch. Harrison bought some holly back from their walk in the park and he has put it in a glitter covered jam jar on the dining table for our Christmas centre piece, clearly Jasmine isn't impressed because she raises her eyebrows at it every time she looks at it, she's only four but she has very strong opinions. Poor Harrison is fifteen months younger and doesn't often manage to impress his big sister.

Mum and dad arrive on time just before lunch, the children are at the window looking out for their grandparents when I hear a cheer, my dad is almost hidden from sight by the enormous tower of presents he is carrying down the path, he is performing quite a balancing act. My mum is armed with a basket of vegetables from her garden and I can imagine she's held them tightly on her lap for the whole journey. I can see luggage is piled high on the back seat of the car which Chris goes out to retrieve.

We spend a lovely afternoon together looking at pictures of my dad's boat following its restoration, now that it's had a new coat of paint and a few mechanical issues fixed she looks as good as new. My mum tells us what she's been up to at her various clubs, I really don't know how she fits it all in. Jasmine can't wait to tell them all about her first term at nursery school, she knows the whole alphabet now and can write her name. Harrison talks about superheroes, none of which my parents have heard of, although because he can't pronounce them all properly it's confusing for most people.

Fortunately, both my mum and dad are thoroughly enchanted with their grandchildren and think that every little thing they do is amazing.

On more than one occasion during the afternoon I'm sure I feel my mum's eyes on me, she's silently watching me like she does when she's worried about me. Jasmine suggests another game of something as soon as the last game has been won; I leave Chris and my parents to oversee that while I make a start on the dinner.

As I knew she would, my mum follows me into the kitchen and demands to know why I look so terrible, she can see through my makeup that I thought I had applied well to disguise the dark shadows that have taken up residency under my eyes. I know I'll probably regret it but I have no choice but to tell her about the dreams, how they are happening more frequently again, she wants to know if I have told Chris, concern is etched deep into her face. I tell her that I haven't told him because there's no point, he doesn't need know, and they are just dreams, nothing that he can control, or fix.

She asks if they are still the same dreams as always, I sigh as I answer her and tell her that "Yes, they are still the same but I can clearly remember different bits each time, sometimes I can see the house, sometimes I'm in a meadow, and sometimes I just feel the sunshine on me then the warmth is replaced by a feeling of intense panic." She puts her arm around my shoulders and leads me over to a chair; she sits opposite me and waits for me to continue. I tell her "Today, I could see the face clearer than ever before. The face belonged to a little boy."

She doesn't know what to say, I've been having these dreams on and off for years, as far back as either one of us can remember. Maybe earlier than that, my mum and dad adopted me when I was three, after my parents died. I don't remember them at all which worried me when I was younger but now I rarely think about being adopted, my parents are Ann and Charlie, they have looked after me almost my whole life and I couldn't have asked for better parents. When I was about nine my mum and dad had told me as much as they could, all they ever knew when they adopted me was that my mother had died in a car crash and there were no living relatives that they could find.

Nobody could ever find any official records on me, my birth was unregistered and I had never attended nursery school or been seen by a doctor. I was wearing a necklace that may or may not have been mine that said Lucy, so that's the name I was given.

They had to work out my age going by a combination of my size and appearance and my physical development, this was difficult because nobody had paid me much attention. I lacked some skills of an average three year old but was well developed in others. I've been told I couldn't talk very well but I could dress myself and I was very sociable, I could make a sandwich but I didn't know my surname or my age, I didn't know where I lived but nothing appeared to worry me. They gave me an approximate age of three based on my growth and size, and because I had been wearing a badge with balloons and cakes on it and I had said it was my birthday they noted my date of birth as the day I was found.

When I turned eighteen I did try to find out who my birth parents were but I didn't get very far. The lady that they think was my mother called herself Butterfly, her real name was Celeste and she had been bought up in the care system so there didn't seem much point delving back further into her past. There was a man with her in the vehicle that night but nobody knew his name and medical records show that he wasn't biologically related to me, I have no clues as to who my father is, or was. I was found sitting by the side of the road not far away from where their vehicle had collided with a tree, killing them both on impact. It's assumed I had been with them and managed to escape unharmed, although I did have few cuts and bruises.

Mum and I work alongside each other in the kitchen preparing a fish pie and a selection of fresh vegetables whilst singing along to the Christmas songs on the radio. Then she takes me by surprise by suddenly hugging me.

"Lucy, it's been such a lovely afternoon, thank you so much for having your dad and me to stay."

She looks quite emotional and I wonder if there's something bothering her, maybe there is something she needs to talk about.

I tell her how much we all love having them both here, it wouldn't be Christmas without them. Then I tell her how much the children have been looking forward to spending this time with them, pleased that it makes her smile. My mum looks quite emotional which is unusual for her. I sense there's more she wants to say but suddenly Lupo comes bounding in closely followed by the children.

Jasmine tells me she is totally starving, she asks if she can help us cook so that she can eat quicker. I tell her that the oven is cooking her dinner as quickly as it can, there's nothing she can do to help us, or to speed it along. Harrison tells me he is starving too, although I'm sure he would say anything Jasmine told him to say.

I suggest they go and get their grandad and daddy to take them and Lupo for a quick walk while my mum and I finish cooking. They turn and run down the hallway while Lupo picks up his lead and trots off after them. A few moments later I hear the front door close and the house falls quiet.

"Don't Mum." I tell her as she looks at me with that quizzical look again, I tell her that I am absolutely fine, I'm sure everybody has strange dreams from time to time. What I don't tell her is that they are beginning to include more detail. Maybe my brain is remembering something from when I was little. I remember when I was about ten years old I had terrible dreams about a book I had been reading at the time, I've always had a vivid imagination. I would read something and then continue it as a dream, sometimes I got confused between the fantasy world I had created in my head and the real world, although it did come in useful in my English writing lessons at school.

I throw her off asking me anymore questions that I don't want to answer by telling her about work and some of the crazy things some of my students have been up to in the science lab, some teenagers are lethal with chemicals and a Bunsen burner, although some of them can cause chaos without the need for any equipment. She tells me about a new friend she's made at one of her clubs whose daughter wants to be a teacher, so we chat about her for a few minutes glad that the attention is off me.

Chris calls out to tell us that they are back at the same moment that a slightly damp Lupo bounds into the kitchen, Chris sets about feeding him while the children go off to wash their hands while mum and I serve our dinner. We are sitting at the dining table which sits at the border between the kitchen and the conservatory. The Christmas tunes are playing softly in the background, the fairy lights on the tree that was a last minute addition to the dining area are casting off a warm golden glow, we all look different in the half light, a bit softer, and blurred around the edges. It's all perfect, except for the earth shattering realisation that I know why I know the face in my dreams.

I can see him now.

Chapter 2 Jack

   I am telling the air next to the phone that "Yes, of course I'm still listening, I will definitely be there on time." On the other end of the phone, my big sister Sophie has been giving me instructions on Christmas day for at least the last ten minutes. Once more she tells me not to be late again, she also reminds me what had happened last year. Actually, I had forgotten about last year, so no wonder she sounds so justifiably cross today. I apologise for that again and tell her that I might have been a few minutes late last year and I've already apologised for that more than once, I promise her faithfully I will be at her house by twelve o'clock at the absolute latest this year, I'll even try to make it for present opening and breakfast, then I tell her to stop worrying.

   She tells me that I said the same thing last year, and reminds me that I wasn't just a few minutes late, I can hear an exasperating sigh down the phone. I do feel bad about last year though, I try to reassure her that although I was slightly later than planned on that occasion she has to remember that I'm a changed man now.

She agrees that now I've got Carrie I do seem to be a bit more mature, Sophie says Carrie certainly brings out the best in me, then comes the question I've been waiting for, she wants to know if Carrie is coming with me for Christmas.

I explain that she is away at the moment, she's spending some time with her sister today, then off to her parents tomorrow to uphold their Christmas Eve tradition of supper and church, then she plans to have breakfast with them Christmas morning and then she's driving back and will hopefully make it in time for Christmas lunch, then we will both stay the night if that's okay with her, although as I'm talking I can almost hear Sophie's happiness travelling down the phone line, I have finally found a girlfriend that my sister approves of.

Sophie tells me that is great news, and with a final warning about my time keeping she is gone. I can imagine that she is dashing off to make everything perfect for our arrival, she wouldn't have worried too much if had it just been me but now she knows Carrie is coming too Sophie will probably be filling the guest room with flowers or something equally as girly. I am actually looking forward to Christmas this year, I'm normally not bothered by it but this year having Carrie makes it feel different, it will be good to catch up with my brother in law Josh too, he's always a good laugh, and he is much more relaxed than Sophie!

Actually, I think as I was almost a day late last year it might be a good idea to set an alarm or two on my phone as a reminder to leave on time, my phone is almost flat so I plug it in to charge so the alarms definitely go off, I can't take any chances of over sleeping again.

Sophie has always been bossy towards me I think fondly, probably because she's the eldest, there's only ten months difference between us but Sophie has always loved being able to say she was the eldest, especially when she had just had a birthday and I had to wait those ten long months to be the same age as her again. I can remember how she would take charge of all of our games when we were children and she would call me baby brother even when I was seven or eight just to wind me up. She still calls me that sometimes now just for the fun of it.

We lived on a farm buried deep in the countryside on the outskirts of a small village, when I think about it we had an idyllic childhood, although at the time we didn't really appreciate it, I wonder if many children do. I'm lucky to have a lot of great memories of being a child, my days were mainly spent with Sophie running through the fields belonging to the farm, I was always pretending to be chased by fearsome dragons or an army of soldiers, my running was spurred on by pretending that the dragon was breathing fire or that an arrow was being fired at me from behind the hedge. Sophie and I spent hours building towers and forts with hay bales, I would find a stick or a broken piece of a branch and pretend it was a mighty sword, a blackberry squashed on it was a gemstone, I would pretend that I was an important knight on a magical mission to save the world from a terrible threat. I always defeated the enemy before dinner time.

There were picnics in hay bale castles with apples that we picked from the trees, there were times we climbed up so high that we thought that we might be able to touch the sky. I remember I even tried to fly off the top of a tower once, we had added bales to the top of the tower from above, lowering them down from a nearby tree, luckily when I was just half way up the tower of hay had collapsed beneath me breaking my fall, I can still remember tumbling to the ground and emerging from a mass of hay to see Sophie's panicked face, it had been her idea that I should try to fly.

Our parents never knew about any of our adventures, they never really understood anything fun. We were always supposed to stay in the garden directly behind the house where we could be seen and play quietly with our toys. We always started off there doing what we were told to do, then we waited until our mother had fallen asleep because that's what she did every afternoon and then we would run off, we knew that our dad would be busy working somewhere but the farm was big enough for us to avoid him. As we got older we would say that we had to go to homework club or some other school related excuse and then we would play one of our games instead, only returning home when the fictional club would have finished and knowing that our dinner was on the way.

I'm jolted out of my walk down memory lane when I suddenly remember I really need to do some Christmas shopping, today is Friday and Christmas is on Sunday. I briefly wonder if I will see my parents at Sophie's house, I didn't think to ask her that but they will probably be there, although it would be much more fun without them, then my conscience kicks in and I feel a bit bad because they are getting old, although I can never remember them looking or acting any younger. Now which shops do gift wrapping? I think to myself as I grab my jacket, check my pocket for the roll of cash that I have just got from a little accounting job on the side and I close the door behind me.

I catch the bus into town and find the jewellery shop that Carrie likes, I take my time choosing something nice for her and then decide to shop for Sophie and my mum as well while I'm in here, I choose a selection of jewellery then the sales assistant puts each item into a box and a gift bag so there's no need for any more wrapping. Pleased with my purchases I dash out of the shop happily whistling to myself just in time to collide with a mate from university that I haven't seen in ages, I'm really not very good at keeping in touch with people.

James tells me he can't stop now but he is meeting Brian for a drink in an hour at the Rose if I want to join them, I tell him it sounds like a great idea, I didn't have anything else planned for today. I tell him I'll be there then check my watch for the time.

I head off to the off licence to get a present for my dad and Josh, it's a shame it doesn't come in a nicer bag but I don't think they will mind, the bottles are clinking together in the plastic carrier bag as I swing it beside me. Then I decide to grab a quick takeaway burger before heading to the pub, from past experience I know that a drink with Brian and James won't be just one drink so it makes sense to eat something first. I go into a fast food outlet, one of the ones Carrie refuses to eat in because it's not considered to be healthy enough for her, I actually feel a little guilty as I bite into my burger whilst hearing her words in my head about fatty foods clogging up my arteries, I wipe the grease from my chin with a scratchy tissue and I promise myself I will eat an apple later to compensate.

As I walk towards the pub I notice that the town is full of happy families, everywhere I look I can see children holding onto their parents hands or skipping alongside them holding onto giant inflatable Santa balloons, whilst licking candy canes or sticky toffee apples. There are carol singers gathered around the tree in the market place singing about the holly and the ivy.

Suddenly I feel an unexpected pang of loneliness. I am missing Carrie much more than I thought I would, but it's not just that, I am shocked to realise that I am actually thinking that I would like to have a real family, I would like a child of my own, well, more than one really. I want to be the kind of parent that I always wanted to have, my parents weren't bad parents but I never felt like they loved me as much as they should, there has always been a distance between us and I know Sophie feels the same, they didn't seem to know what they should have been doing with us when we were growing up. They never took us on holidays or trips to anywhere fun, not even trips to the beach in the summer time. My dad just wanted to work while my mum drank their homemade cider and slept quite a lot, although she always made sure that Sophie and I were well fed.

I want to have my own children to play games with and to teach to ride a bike, I want to do den building and story times, in the summer time we could go camping and toast marshmallows on the fire, we could make sandcastles on the beach, visit the zoos and theme parks. I think I really need to have a serious chat with Carrie about our future plans, hopefully she will feel the same way.

It is great fun catching up with my mates in our old haunt, we spend hours reminiscing about the good old times and the pranks that we got up to at university, it's amazing that we got away with some of the things we did, especially the time we covered some of the seats in the lecture hall with itching powder and sat sprinkling it down the backs of the people seated in front of us, poor John Hughes was red and itchy all week.

James tells me that he has just got married for the second time and is trying very hard to be a good husband this time, although, he says he doesn't really know what he did wrong in his first marriage, but he managed to lose his house and half of his bank balance along with his ex. Brian is still looking for someone who will put up with his compulsive neatness and his strict fitness regime, he's a great mate but he sounds impossible to live with.

Somehow, before we know it we've all had far too much to drink and it is closing time. Brian and James share a cab home but I live in the opposite direction and I decide that a brisk walk back home will do me good.

As we leave the pub I totally forget about my bags of Christmas shopping that I put safely under the table hours ago. I have also forgotten that the street lights go off just after the pubs close so it might take me a bit longer than I originally thought to get home. I'm still thinking about the possibility of starting a family with Carrie, and then I smile to myself and dig my hands a bit deeper into my coat pockets in an attempt to keep warm as I begin the long walk home. I'm luckily oblivious to the turn my life is about to take.

Chapter 3 Lucy

I sleep peacefully for the first time in weeks and I wake up to find the watery winter sun is creeping through the gap in the curtains and warming my face. I stretch out my limbs that feel strangely heavy and fill my lungs with a deep breath as I open my eyes. As my brain wakes up and springs into motion I remember it is Christmas Eve and we've got lots of nice things planned for today.

Then within an instant and without warning, I am winded. I can see him again, not the little boy this time but a man. A man who is clearly in a great deal of pain, he appears to be in a hospital bed, my blood is running cold and I can sense his pain, I don't know who he is but I know with absolute certainty that he is called Callum.

"What is it Lucy?" Mumbles a sleepy Chris.

I'm sat up in bed now and I didn't realise it but I've woken Chris, worse still I find I'm crying, great big sobs are tearing through my body. I try to calm myself because he looks terrified but the feelings are too intense to ignore, I can't hold it back, the tears are falling and a cold sweat is running down my back.

"There's a man and I can see that he is hurt, he's in my dream, but it can't be a dream because I'm awake." I manage to tell Chris between my sobs. I can't make sense of it, my brain feels both fuzzy and on high alert. I reach for a tissue and dab at my tears, my eyes are stinging. I tell Chris "I don't know what all this is but I know that he, Callum, is alone, he's in a lot of pain, I don't understand it but I know without a doubt he is definitely called Callum." Then I lie back down and hug the pillow tightly to me as though it's my life raft.

"Okay." Says Chris although I'm sure there are a hundred thoughts racing through his head right now and okay probably isn't one of them.

"I'm as confused as you are." I tell him a few moments later. "I don't know anyone called Callum but somehow I know that is his name, and I also know that he is in a hospital." I don't dare tell him that I feel as though I am feeling Callum's pain, he is already looking at me like I'm crazy, I'm trying hard not to think that he might be right.

"Okay." Says Chris again, with slightly more conviction in his voice this time. He is stroking my back and I'm not sure if it's in an effort to soothe me or himself. This isn't the first time I've had one of these occurrences as we call them. A few years ago we met a lady in a country pub whilst we were on holiday miles away from home, she was serving behind the bar and asked me how old my baby was, Jasmine was just six months old at that time and I was a newly proud mother so we chatted for a while, she went to introduce herself but I remember saying that I already knew her, she was called Polly. Chris said I must have overheard someone else in the pub saying it, but I didn't, I just knew her. I'd known she would be there the minute we parked in the car park. The same way I knew I'd been to a lake that we saw on a TV documentary, I had told Chris there was a butterfly farm nearby, he looked it up on the internet and I was right, there was a butterfly farm just a few miles away, a lucky guess he said. But, as I said, sometimes I just know things and I can't explain how, maybe they are simply buried childhood memories.

This morning is Christmas Eve and I don't want the day to be spoiled so I somehow manage to convince Chris that I am fine, although I'm no way near to believing it myself. I tell him to have another half an hour in bed while I go and start on breakfast, I need some time to myself to try and work through what has just happened. We've woken up later than normal but the children are thankfully still asleep. Lupo meets me at the bottom of the stairs and sensing my distress he comes up close to me and as I bend down to ruffle his ears he leans his silky head on my shoulder and I bury my head into his fur, I cling onto him as I start to cry again, all I can see in my mind's eye is the mysterious Callum.

In the kitchen I turn up the radiator as far as I can and then I switch the tree lights on, it isn't enough so I light as many candles as I can find to make the room feel warmer because I'm so unbelievably cold. Soon, the aroma of freshly brewed coffee is filing the air, I've also reheated come croissants and pain au chocolat, and made a fruit salad with some strawberries and melon. Lupo bounds back in from the garden bringing with him an icy blast of outside air that seems to cling onto my skin. The sky this morning is a clear brittle blue, holding the threat of snow in its clutches.

I begin taking breakfast over to the table as the rest of my family appear. They are all in a happy Christmas mood so I try as hard as I can to bury Callum at the back of my mind until I'm alone again.

The morning passes by quickly; my dad plays superheroes with Harrison using blankets tied onto their shoulders as cloaks. Meanwhile, my mum teaches an eager Jasmine how to make her own bread for our lunch today; she has great fun kneading the dough. Chris and I potter about and join in the fun.

However, throughout the games and laughter I'm still thinking of Callum. I have to find him.

I grab my phone and manage to disappear upstairs unnoticed, I have a plan. I start phoning around all of the hospitals in the region asking if a Callum has been bought in, without a surname some of the people I speak to are reluctant to help me, so, I make a note to call those ones back later when their shifts have changed. As I start to widen my search area I hear footsteps outside the bedroom door, I realise I've been up here for just over an hour, Chris won't understand this at all so I hide my phone under my pillow and lay down pretending to be asleep. The guilt overwhelms me as he sits down next to me and tenderly strokes my face to wake me up. I hope the trembling of my body doesn't betray me because I become nervous when I lie. I let a moment pass before I swallow hard to stop the tears from forming and I cautiously open my eyes.

"Hey you," He says "Your mum wondered what you were doing up here, I thought you'd be tired after this morning's events so I persuaded her to leave you to rest for a bit."

I sense he's about to say something else so in an effort to avoid any further conversations about my mental state, I jump up telling him that as I didn't eat much at breakfast I'm starving now and I need to eat, although I don't honestly think I've fooled him it's the best I can do right now. I take his hand and pull him to his feet without making eye contact, and then I follow him down to lunch wondering if I'll be able to get past my mother's inquisition.

My daughter is very proud of her first attempt at baking bread and she did a great job, between the six of us we have eaten two large loaves and half a cheese board, washed down with a glass of red wine that my dad said we needed to have with the cheese. I've barely begun digesting my food when my mum jumps up from her seat.

"Okay boys," She says looking at dad and Chris "You two can tidy up and look after the little ones while Lucy and I walk into town for some more cheese."

I almost choke on my wine, I tell her that I think I've got loads of cheese, the fridge is almost at bursting point, but she insists you can never have too much cheese. She leaves little room for any argument when she tells me to go and get my coat on and be ready to go in two minutes, she's already gone to find her coat leaving me with little choice but to do as I have been told, I feel like I'm five years old again, although I'm not sure her excuse to get me out alone is solely cheese based which makes me a bit nervous.

We've barely closed the front door before her barrage of questions begins "Lucy, you look worse than you did yesterday, is it Chris? Are you two having problems? Is it money? Are you..."

"Mum stop." I tell her "Chris and I are fine, we don't have problems between us, no money problems or any other kind of problems, everything is great, and it's my favourite time of year so will you just stop worrying." She listens and raises her eyebrows but doesn't push the matter. My shoulders are sagging under the weight of my lie but there's little point in her worrying about me, it won't change anything, she's here to have an enjoyable Christmas with her family, not to worry about her daughter who occasionally sees images of people she doesn't know.

We walk in silence for a few moments then she abruptly stops walking and turns to face me, she tells me that although I might be able to fool other people surely I've learnt by now that I can't fool her, then she does this trick that she has mastered where she looks deep into my eyes and asks me again "Are you alright?" and I blink and look away because I'm lying to her. She's done this to me ever since I was a little girl, it's impossible to look her directly in the eye and tell a lie. It's a trick I've used at school on my students and occasionally on own children, it never fails.

So I tell her "I had a dream, well, more like a vision really of a man called Callum who is in a hospital somewhere, that's it really, now let's get the cheese you so desperately wanted and go home before it snows." And I turn away from her and walk off.

After a few moments I turn and retrace my steps because she hasn't moved. I can see she has no idea what to say in response to my outburst, she is probably wishing I had money problems instead then she would be able to help me. Confusion is written all over her face and for the first time that I can remember she is speechless. I feel bad for snapping at her when I can see she is trying to find the right thing to say but she just can't put any words together, if it wasn't such an odd situation it would be quite comical.

In an attempt to lighten the mood again I link my arm through hers and suggest stopping for some mulled wine after we've stocked up on the cheese. She knows what I'm trying to do and squeezes my arm as she kisses my forehead. We silently agree not to mention the episode again and just enjoy each other's company.

We go to my favourite delicatessen for the cheese that we don't really need, then I take my mum to a pub that I know will have a roaring fire to warm us up while we have our mulled wine. We talk about nothing of any importance while we sit there then she talks to an elderly couple who come in with their dog, Mum knows her from years ago. I sit back and listen to them chatting although nothing goes in, my mind is too full but I appreciate her giving me a bit of breathing space.

As we are leaving the pub it starts to snow, just a few magical feathery flakes twirling in the wind, then floating along in the breeze and mingling with the sound of bells in the distance, reminding us that Christmas is almost upon us.

Back home my house is in absolute chaos, but my children look ridiculously happy, they pop their heads up from the den they have made in the middle of the room using the sofa cushions and a few old blankets. Chris and my dad are lying on the floor nearby, they both look totally exhausted.

I tell them all that if we still want to make the carol concert in the church tonight I suggest we tidy up and have a nap before we eat. That last part about the nap was directed at Jasmine and Harrison but my dad and Chris seem keener than the children do to have a snooze. Within minutes the room is miraculously restored to its original state and my mum is on the sofa with a sleeping Harrison on her lap. Jasmine goes up for a nap but makes us all promise to wake her in an hour.

"Are you okay with Harrison laying on you Mum? I can scoop him up if you'd rather?"

"No dear, I'm fine, anyway, if you move him he might wake up! I'm fine here."

"Okay, thanks Mum. I just have a couple of calls to make. I'll be back down soon."

"Who do you have to phone on Christmas Eve? everywhere will be shut now, and I thought you young people did all your communicating on those fancy phones you all have that ping things to each other without the need for talking."

She's got me now, I'm not sure if that was her intention or a lucky intervention. "Mum, remember Harrison is asleep," I say whispering to her. "I was just going to make a few calls to some hospitals to see if I could track this Callum down." Then I can see she is about to launch into a lecture so I point to the sleeping form of my son on her lap in an attempt to silence her.

"Lucy, that really is most crazy, I really think..." But before she can finish her sentence I blow her a kiss and leave the room.

In the sanctuary of my conservatory I feel calmer, how is it a different room can make your moods shift? I lean back in my favourite chair and settle against the cushions before closing my eyes. I feel my limbs becoming weightless and my mind gives itself over to nothingness.

I open my eyes when I hear a noise coming from outside that startles me, I must have fallen asleep because I can suddenly see him again as I'm jolted back to reality. This time when I wake up I'm not scared though, I'm determined. I put my coat on and go outside for some privacy. I sit on the bench at the bottom of the garden under the shelter of an apple tree and take out my phone.

The first number I dial is one that I had already tried earlier and got a very unhelpful lady. This time it's answered on the second ring.

"Molly speaking, how can I help?"

"Hello there, how are you?" I reply. I'm trying a friendlier approach this time.

"Oh, hello, I'm good thanks how can I help you?" She sounds very young.

I try to phrase it right but I'm not sure I succeed when I say "Well, I know this might seem a bit odd but I'm looking for a man called Callum, I think he came in late last night or early this morning, after some kind of accident."

"Okay," She says cheerily down the phone "Let me check for you, can I take his surname please?"

"Ah, that's a bit of a problem, I don't have it." I can almost hear her rolling her eyes at me now.

"So, you don't know the surname of your friend, that doesn't make much sense." She's drumming her pencil against something now, clearly getting impatient with me.

No, it doesn't make sense I think to myself, I realise now how hopeless this is. Unless... "Well, the thing is, we only met last night, we spent the evening together and he didn't show up this morning where we were supposed to meet so I need to know if he's been hurt."

I can hear the curiosity in her voice now when she says "This is a bit unusual. Have you considered the possibility that he just didn't want to see you again? Or maybe he's at home hung over and has forgotten all about you?"

What am I supposed to say now? If I tell her I've had visions of him she will think I'm totally crazy and hang up, or transfer me to a psychiatrist, so instead I tell her "I have considered all those options but I really think he's hurt, could you just check please, I can give you a full description of him."

"Ok, go ahead, what does this man of yours look like?"

"He has very blonde hair, he is well built with a kind face, I think he has blue eyes and is in his early to mid thirties."

I think she's enjoying playing detective now, she tells me she will have a look, then I am put on hold and classical music fills my ears, while I wait I say a silent prayer. After a few minutes she's back on the line.

"I'm sorry but I can't see anyone that could be the man you are looking for. We had one Callum but I really don't think he is the one for you, he doesn't match your description."

I tell her that he could be, after all, I can't be sure of anything I've just told her, I ask her to tell me which ward he is on and I'll be straight in to see him.

She giggles slightly as she tells me that this Callum is eighty-nine years old, he came in with his wife early yesterday evening after they had glued their hands together whilst trying to repair an old jug.

I agree that he probably isn't the Callum I am looking for, I thank her for looking. Then I ask if I could leave my number with her just in case another Callum does come in. She says it's impossible to say no as its Christmas time, I repeat my number twice to make sure she's got it right and thank her again. She tells me she hopes I find him if he's that special. I hope I do to. I'm about to dial the next number when...

"So," Says Chris, "Do you want to tell me about that?"

Oh god, I've got no idea how long he's been standing there, I'm really not sure what to tell him, so I ask him how long he's been there, he might not have heard anything odd, maybe I can rescue the situation, make up something about a friend in trouble, maybe I can say Beth has a problem because she's always getting herself into odd situations. But he tells me he followed me out here, how did I not see him? I'm angry now, I feel like he was trying to catch me out,

"If you have just heard everything that I said why are you asking?" I shout at him "I told you about that man I saw in my dream or whatever it was, I don't expect you to understand but I need to know that he is okay." I make to move past him to go back into the house but he grabs my arm and holds me still.

"Lucy, it's Christmas Eve, and instead of enjoying time with your family you want to spend your time hiding in the garden in the freezing cold phoning hospitals looking for a total stranger, who may or may not exist, am I right? Or did I miss anything out?"

Oh god, he's right, I hate it when he's right, I'm losing the plot. I really don't want to fall out with him over this, especially at Christmas time. In an effort to make amends I tell him that I realise it sounds a bit crazy when he says it like that but he doesn't understand how important this is to me.

"I thought your family was important to you." He throws back at me.

"You know you are." I say as he draws me closer to him.

We stay linked together like that for a few moments and I realise he is right. I'm letting a dream come before the people that really matter. Hand in hand we go back inside to see if Harrison has woken up yet. He hasn't, his little body is still curled up fast asleep, his eyelashes are fluttering in tune to his dream and my mum has dozed off too.

Dad comes in with Lupo who looks like he's been rolling in snow so I fetch the towel we keep for him and dry him off as he lays in front of the fire. As the logs start to crackle Lupo barks and wakes everyone up, although I realise it's time we were waking up and eating anyway. There's a beef and vegetable stew bubbling away in the slow cooker and the rest of the homemade bread to go with it.

I go and wake Jasmine as the others get the table ready for dinner. She's beaten me to it though, as I go into her room she's jumping up telling me she is so very hungry so it's totally impossible to sleep, although I can see from the way her hair is stuck to the side of her face that she has been asleep. I hug her close for a moment, inhaling her sleepy smell.

"Well that's good, I'm glad you are hungry because dinner is ready." I tell her.

It seems they worked up an appetite den building because they all have second helpings of the stew.

"Who Clump Mummy?" Harrison suddenly asks me, we had been talking about when to leave for church.

"Pardon, what do you mean? Who's who?" I ask him.

"Clump, you say Clump." Harrison replies trying very hard with his words.

Mum and dad are looking at each other as though they are looking at ghosts, I'm not sure who to talk to first, my son or my parents, because they are each looking at me with uncertainty written on their faces, waiting for me to answer.

"Clump, you said Clump Mummy, Clump in the hosapotal."

I see a look passing between my mum and dad that I can't read, then very slowly, my dad puts down his knife and fork and hesitantly turns to me.

"Lucy, you used to talk about Clump when you were little, until now I hadn't thought of him in years, but don't you remember? Clump was your imaginary friend."

The room is spinning, I feel like I'm in a vacuum that I can't escape from, the people in front of me have become shadows and the noise is closing in on me creating a relentless pressure in my head that I have no control over. I can hear the frantic thumping of my heart and the blood rushing through my veins, I try to steady myself as much as I can and then I run out through the French doors into the garden, hungrily taking in deep breaths of the frosty air. I'm hot and sweating but I'm shivering at the same time and it has nothing to do with the fact that I'm outside in the snow wearing just a T-shirt.

I'm startled when I feel a weight on my shoulders and I let out an involuntary scream, I'm waving my arms around trying to defend myself before I realise it's the blanket from the sofa in the conservatory, Chris is wrapping me in it, he must have grabbed it on his way out. He is hugging me tightly while trying but failing to inject some warmth into my body. Mum and Dad appear at my side too.

"Where are the children?"

"We've put one of their films on for them for a few minutes, don't worry, they're fine, what's going on Lucy? You look like you're about to pass out."

My thoughts are travelling at a million miles an hour, I try to get things straight in my head before voicing them out loud, I am remembering my imaginary friend now but he wasn't called Clump. I can't believe I'd forgotten all about him. Harrison must get his slow developing speech from me. I steady my breathing and stand silent and still, I'm making sure my memories are accurate. I am pushing my feet down into the ground trying to anchor myself to the real world, and then I take a few steps away from them all and take another round of deep steadying breaths. After a moment I turn back to face them.

"I think maybe he's back and all grown up," I tell them with a tremor in my voice. "My imaginary friend was called Callum."

Chapter 4 *Celeste* age 5

My tummy hurts, it's really dark so I've gone to bed but the pain in my tummy is getting worse, I can't sleep because it hurts so much. My mummy and daddy have got their friends round again but I'm not ever allowed to see any of their friends, I did sneak a peek from a crack in my door one night but the only man I did see looked very scary, his skin looked funny, a bit like he had been face painted, and then let it all smudge together. I'm really hungry so before the people all came I asked for something to eat but my mummy said there wasn't anything, she said she would try to find me something in the morning. My tummy keeps on growling, it sounds like a monster.

There is a lot of noise in our little flat so I put my pillow over my head, I can still hear the music and the people but it sounds different now, the words have gone and now it just sounds like banging, I close my eyes and pretend it is the waves of the sea that I can hear, I pretend that I am on a beach. I wish I really was on the beach.

My grandma took me to the beach last summer, I like my grandma, she bought me chips and then we had an ice-cream cone as well, it was the best day that I have ever had. She even let me put my feet in the sea, we jumped over the waves as they landed on the sand, then when I stood still my feet sunk down into the wet sand, it tickled when I wiggled my toes, we giggled when I told grandma that. I wish I could go to the beach with my grandma again but when I asked my mummy about it she said I can't because grandma isn't here anymore, when I asked where grandma had gone my daddy said she had gone to live in heaven, I was going to ask my mummy where heaven was but she started to cry so I didn't ask any more questions.

I think I must have been asleep for a little while because my pillow isn't over my head anymore, it has fallen onto the floor. I can hear lots of shouting again and I feel a little bit scared. I reach my arm out into the cold air to pick up my pillow and put it back over my head and then I pull the duvet up too, then I hide again and think of the beach while I try to make myself go back to sleep. I try to make myself dream of nice things but it's so hard when the monster in my tummy keeps growling and swimming around.

Chapter 5 1985

"Sophie, look here sweetheart, this is Jackson, he is your new baby brother, isn't he the most adorable baby boy? You two will have so much fun together as you grow up, you'll always have each other."

"Come on Susan, she's only ten months old herself, she's got no idea what you are talking about and she couldn't answer you even if she wanted to."

"Of course I know that Peter, I'm just so happy with our perfect little family. I honestly feel like I am the luckiest woman in the world to have two beautifully perfect children and it's all down to you. I am determined to do everything in my power to make sure they grow up happy and healthy, I honestly never imagined I could ever be so happy."

"I know you are going to be a wonderful mother to him, just as you are to Sophie, and I promise to do all I can to help you with them both, although with the farm to run I am worried about how much time you are on your own. I wish we were making a bit more money so I could take on someone to help me, but there's just no way that I can afford to do that yet."

"Oh, I know that Peter, but I'm sure as the crops become more established and we get a regular trade for the vegetables it will become a profitable business. You've worked so hard the last few years and the farm is already becoming unrecognisable. I'm so proud of all the hard work you do for us. It will all come right in the end, I just know it."

"Stop being soppy woman; let's have some more cake to celebrate this little one being born shall we?" And he goes to the kitchen to get some more of Susan's special fruit cake, and maybe a small whisky to go with it he thinks.

Peter can't quite believe the turn his life has taken. Three years ago he had met Susan at the local pub and now here they are, married with two children to raise while trying to make a success of the run down old farm his grandparents had left to him. He was under no illusions that the next few years were going to be anything but easy; he knew how hard he would have to work to make a success of Lavender farm.

It had been Susan's idea that alongside the corn they grew in the fields, and a few animals that they kept for dairy, they should start growing more vegetables. The plan was to have enough to sell to the local businesses and to take some to the local markets each week. Susan had been right though because it was proving increasingly difficult to keep up with the demand, especially as he was doing all the work alone. Susan's pregnancies had not been planned, the plan had been for her to tend to the vegetable gardens and maybe make some homemade cakes and other homemade produce to sell at the markets alongside the vegetables. Clearly fate had a different path in store for them.

He really needed to get the accounts up to date to see if he could afford some help, even if it was just for a few mornings each week to begin with. There was also an apple orchard that had been seriously neglected; those apples would definitely sell at the market if he could get them picked. Maybe if the children had a nap and Susan were to have any spare time, then maybe she could turn some of the apples into jams or chutneys. There was a lot of potential and he couldn't help but wish, just a little bit, that his children could have waited a few years to be born.

He cut himself an extra thick slice of fruitcake and went back in to see his wife and children who were all fast asleep. With a heavy sigh he sat down to join them deciding that it might be a wise idea to catch forty winks while he could, so he downed his whisky, settled back into his worn old chair, and closed his eyes.

Over the next few months Susan did all she could to help Peter on the farm. Sophie would play nearby in a playpen outside and Jackson slept peacefully in his pram, or sat up and watched while Susan worked on the vegetable gardens, she could see how tired Peter was becoming so she did all she could to help out. She had even managed to persuade him to turn one of the empty fields into a campsite to generate some extra income. All they'd had to do was to get a small bank loan so they could have amenities block built; they would easily pay that off in no time once the campers came. Peter wasn't keen on that idea at all in the beginning but the field was a good few minutes' walk from the house so they wouldn't be losing any of their privacy. In the end he had agreed that the field in question was perfect, there was a small stream running past the bottom of the field and he had even put rope swings in two of the trees and built a brick barbecue. He had been quite frankly shocked at how much money people would pay to pitch a tent in an empty field for the night. As much he hated the thought of sharing Lavender farm with strangers he couldn't turn down that kind of money. They were due to open to the public in a few months time around the Easter holiday season and they were almost fully booked already. Maybe their luck was about to change for the better.

Chapter 6 Lucy

We make it to the church just in time for the beginning of the service, luck is on our side because we even manage to find an empty pew, we all squeeze in before unwinding our scarves and shaking out stray snowflakes from our hair. There are groups of children from two of the local primary schools here tonight, they each perform a nativity scene and sing a variety of traditional carols, although I had never heard their version of Little Donkey before, the vicar looked a bit confused too. There was a sticky moment during the first performance when King Herod got struck by stage fright but his mother was able to get him to carry on by sitting behind him on the stage. He thoroughly enjoyed his applause at the end and all of his stage fright soon vanished as he took a bow.

There is a beautiful bunch of Christmassy flowers tied to the end of each pew, the rich reds and glossy greenery is generously studded with golden pine cones, and deep red berries, larger matching versions stand at the front of the church on either side of the altar, a glistening tree decked out in red and gold is towering above the choir as they close the service with a pitch perfect rendition of Silent Night. It truly is a beautiful evening that reminds us all of the true meaning of Christmas. I almost feel guilty that I only ever come to church at Christmas time, or for weddings and funerals.

At the end of the service we wrap ourselves up again and file out of the church into the crisp night air. Harrison says that he is cold and he is looking a bit sleepy so Chris hoists him up onto his shoulders which makes him giggle, Jasmine is happy swinging off the arms of her grandparents and seeing how high she can jump. I smile to myself as I watch my family, I love them so much it hurts, but if they could read my mind they'd be horrified to know I can't forget Callum, my mind has been focused on him during the service, why has my childhood imaginary friend come back now? I'm almost thirty three years old, what's wrong with me? I'm hoping it's just down to tiredness but I think I'm being naive.

My dad is singing carols to Jasmine and the walk home feels oddly refreshing. Just as we near our road we pass the a new coffee shop that transforms to a wine bar in the evenings, it only opened a few weeks ago, the windows are steamed up and a fuzzy orange glow is coming from within.

"Hot chocolate, hot chocolate shop." Squeals a very excited little Jasmine.

"Ah yes, I bet they do a lovely mulled wine as well, come on everyone, my treat." Says my mum and before we can reply she's halfway through the door.

The waitress tells us a table has just been vacated upstairs, so up we go, the stairs are a bit narrow and as I follow my dad I realise he's looking a bit frail, I hope he is alright. It scares me to think about my parents getting old, they are both only a few years off seventy now although they don't normally look it.

The hot chocolate that is set in front of Jasmine must have a whole carton of whipped cream sitting on top of it, along with chocolate shavings, marshmallows, and a flake, she digs in eagerly with a spoon. Harrison wanted a hot milk, he always chooses milk if it's on the menu. The rest of us drink from tall glass mugs filled to the brim with mulled wine, topped with cinnamon sticks and warm slices of orange and lemon, it tastes and smells amazing. As a special treat mum has also ordered a baked camembert and warm bread, the cheese oozes from its casing and tastes just as delicious as it looks.

The children have found some colouring books so they are happy. I'm humming silent night in my head while surreptitiously checking my phone to see if any of the hospitals have called me back, but unfortunately they haven't. I feel my eyes growing heavy and realise I'm almost falling asleep. Chris is talking to my dad about his boat while mum is colouring in a picture of a farmyard with the children. I stretch my back and legs out and try unsuccessfully to stifle a yawn.

"Thank you Mum for such a lovely treat, but it's getting late now so I really think it's time we headed home."

"But Mummy, I haven't finished my picture." Whines Jasmine.

"Mummy is right Jasmine; it's time to go home now. If you are too tired in the morning you'll sleep in and miss out on Christmas day tomorrow." Chuckles Chris.

Her little face looks horror struck and she is the first one wrapped up and ready to go this time, I decide not to tell her she's buttoned her coat up wrong. She's bounding down the stairs leading us outside where we find a thick covering of snow. Cars have turned white and the path is indistinguishable from the road, thankfully we only have a short walk ahead. I grab onto my dad's arm and hold Jasmines hand on my other side, I give Chris a nod in my mum's direction, he gets the message and holds Harrison on one side while steadying my mum with his other arm.

We are home within minutes where the welcoming warmth of the house wraps itself around us diffusing the cold. We all feel suddenly sleepy and decide it's time to head up to bed. Tomorrow is going to be a busy day.

Chapter 7 Celeste age 7

Today I am feeling sad because the children at school have started being unkind to me, they say that I smell funny and that my hair is yucky. There is a new little boy called Tom, he said he will be my friend if I want him to be, the other children are mean to him too, and they point at his ears and laugh. I asked him what the thing is that he has on both of his ears and he told me it is a special machine that helps him to hear because his ears don't work very well. I think that the machines sound very clever so I don't know why the other children think it's so funny. Tom is a bit quiet but I don't mind because it's nice to have a friend.

Tonight I asked my mummy if she thought I smelled funny, she came really close to me and wiggled her nose, then she said I did smell a bit off, then she laughed too, I'm getting really fed up with everyone laughing at me. Mummy said I could have a bath if I wanted to make myself smell of roses, I don't know what roses are but they sound nice so I told her that yes please, I really want a bath.

I asked mummy what roses are and she laughed again, I followed her to the bathroom and watched as she filled the bath up with water, then she told me to get in. The water is so cold, colder than the sea was at the beach, she can see that I am shivering but she said there's nothing in the meter for hot water but I didn't ask what that meant, I just wanted to get out of the cold bath. Mummy wouldn't let me out of the water until she had washed my hair, so I sat there in the cold water with my arms wrapped around my knees trying to keep warm while my mummy washed my hair. She made it all bubbly and I think I could smell apples, then she used a jug to water the bubbles off my hair, I watched as they floated away in the water. I got out of the cold water and my mummy wrapped me in a towel and rubbed it a bit to dry me, the towel was scratchy on my skin but I didn't tell her that because it was nice being with my mummy. I think she needs a bath because she smells a bit funny too, I am about to tell her that but then my daddy calls for her to hurry up. She tells me to go to bed.

But I don't go to bed, I creep into her room and borrow one of her hairbrushes, and then I brush my hair until the knots are all gone, it hurts a bit but I keep on going until my hair hangs straight down my back. I think I will try to sleep on my back tonight to make my hair stay flat, like the other girls hair, then maybe they will like me, and then I can tell them that I smell of roses.

Chapter 8 Lucy

I wake up feeling rested and relaxed, but then as I roll over to look at the time my dream comes rushing back to me. I don't know when I first conjured up Callum as a child but he was in my dream again last night, or maybe it is a memory that I had buried in the past as I had grown up. Callum and I were playing in a big grassy meadow, I'll have to ask mum and dad where that was, I can see myself now, I'm sitting on the grass threading a daisy chain, making Callum bring me more daisies, I'm not sure how that could have happened that now that I've discovered he was made up, I must only have been about three or four, it's funny the fragments of our lives that our brain chooses to either remember or discard.

I'm alerted to a shuffling noise downstairs so after wrapping myself in my dressing gown I go down to investigate, I hope Lupo isn't up to mischief. The first Christmas we had him he managed to escape from the kitchen where he always sleeps at night, he had knocked the Christmas tree over and chewed his way through half of the Christmas presents before we had heard what he was doing.

I needn't have worried today though, in the kitchen I find my mum softly singing we wish you a merry Christmas to herself, and poor Lupo is hiding under the table looking bemused. Firstly I wish her a happy Christmas while giving her a hug before bending down to do the same to Lupo.

"Ah, Lucy, you startled me, what are you doing up so early?"

"I could ask you that same question Mum; you've already done almost all of the vegetables."

"I'm a creature of habit, I woke up and couldn't lay idle so I thought I'd make myself useful, are you okay love?"

"I'm good thanks Mum, I know what you are thinking, and I'm fine, really."

"So, no more strange vision dream type things then?" She asks me.

"Well, as I was waking up I did remember a bit of a dream, but it wasn't scary this time. I think because now I know it was just my mind delving into the past playing tricks on me it's not worrying me, I'm just curious now, trying to piece it all together."

"Oh, that is good Lucy, your dad and I were getting very worried about you. Maybe it's now that you have children of your own you are remembering things from your own childhood that you thought you had forgotten about a long time ago."

I don't like to tell her I've had thoughts of Callum on and off for years now, long before my children were born, I decide its best to keep that to myself.

"Let's make some coffee shall we Mum?"

"Lovely idea, I think that mulled wine last night was extra strong."

"That's probably because you had three of them!" Says my Dad from behind us, he still looks a bit sleepy as he looks gratefully at the coffee pot.

I suggest we take it through to the lounge so we can turn the tree lights on and enjoy the last few minutes of calm before the little people get up, they agree and follow me through, my mum is still singing and she looks very happy.

Hospital

In the hospital there is a lot of talk and speculation about who the mystery man might be, the nurses all agree that it is odd that he's been in there over twenty-four hours now without being identified, they are all saying that surely someone must have missed him by now. What puzzles them most is the fact that he was found with nothing to identify him, what was he doing out walking with no wallet and no phone? Unless he was mugged after being hit by the car, but that's unlikely as he was still wearing his watch. They all agree that he is very good looking, surely he has a girlfriend or a wife, or even a family member to miss him, and it's very strange that someone hasn't claimed him by now. It would be nice if someone could be here with him when he regains consciousness.

Wendy says she will talk to the police again to see if he matches the description of any new missing person reports they've had.

Sophie

"Arrah! This is just so typical of him, how hard is it to get in the car and drive for half an hour and turn up here for lunch?" I'm asking Josh but he doesn't share my concern, he tells me to calm down, and then he reminds me that Jack is always late, that's not what I wanted to hear, this year he promised he would be here and I actually believed him. Then Josh tells me that lunch still won't be for a few hours so technically

Jack isn't even late yet, if he was here this early he would be surprised, I'm not sure if he is being serious or deliberately winding me up so I tell him that I would appreciate it if he would stop defending my idiot brother.

He wraps me in a hug and says that he is not defending Jack, he is simply telling me to stop stressing about it. If he's late, he's late, we can't change that, and I suppose he's right. We take a glass of fizz through to the living room where Daisy has been entertaining my parents for the last half an hour. Daisy might only be five but she's a master at handling her grandparents, I wish I knew how she did it, I've known them all my life and I still don't know how to make them happy, it's Christmas day and they still haven't cracked a smile. If Jack doesn't show up again this year I vow I will never forgive him.

Daisy has unwrapped all of her Christmas presents, her favourite one is her new bike. It's painted a metallic pink and it has purple stars clipped onto the wheel spokes, it is exactly the same as the one in the picture that she posted to Santa. She is desperate to ride it so she is very annoyed that the paths are covered in snow. She's keeping herself busy with colouring books and jigsaw puzzles but every few minutes she is looking outside to see if the snow has melted.

Josh catches Daisy looking outside again and he suggests they all wrap up and go outside to build a snowman while I'm busy cooking, Daisy happily agrees while my parents try to find reasons to stay inside in the warm, Daisy refuses to take no for an answer, soon they are all outside collecting handfuls of snow and attempting to build a snowman. Jack would be rolling around the floor in laughter if he could see our mum and dad out there, Daisy has just thrown a snowball at my dad and my mum is now hiding behind the rotting conifer tree. I don't ever remember them building a snowman with Jack and me as children.

Josh is right, it's not even eleven o'clock yet so Jack isn't late yet, I knew he wouldn't actually make it for breakfast but deep down I'd hoped that he might, I'm trying not to stress about the time but I just hope he is here before Carrie arrives.

Lucy

Mummy, Mummy, Mummy," Cries Jasmine whilst bounding down the stairs at break neck speed "It's finally here, it's Christmas day!"

I wrap my arms tightly around her and as I feel her squirming to get away I tickle her until she is rolling around on the rug and giggling, I hear a noise behind me and see that Chris and Harrison have joined us as well, they are both still in their pyjamas. I go over to give them a both big hug, and a Christmas kiss.

"Mummy, did Stanta come?" Asks my little boy, I remind myself that I really should get some help for Harrisons speech. I tell him that yes; of course Santa came because he has been such a good boy all year. His face lights up when he sees the piles of presents spilling out from under the tree. I tell everyone to come and sit down while I bring us all a little bit of breakfast through to munch on while we are opening presents. Jasmine says she wants to open her presents first, because nobody wants silly breakfast on Christmas day.

Chris never lets anything come between him and food so he tells her we definitely do need something to eat and that waiting another five minutes isn't the end of the world, but she doesn't agree and her little face looks very cross, she looks so cute it's hard not to laugh. I'm reminded that Callum used to make a face like that, and then I'm annoyed with myself that my thoughts keep going back to him. A few minutes later I'm carrying through a tray with coffee, juice, a massive plate of toast and a mug of hot milk for Harrison. Lupo has fallen asleep in front of the fire, he is snoring quietly and I imagine he is dreaming that he is running in a big green meadow chasing squirrels.

Chris looks just the part today, he is wearing his Santa hat and he is sitting in front of the tree sorting out the presents, he has done this every year now since the children came along.

"Ho, Ho, Ho, who would like the first present?" He says in his terrible fake Santa voice.

He is answered by a chorus of "Me me me Daddy." So laughing he gives them both a present at the same time. The next hour passes by in a blur of wrapping paper and excitement. The last present under the tree is one I hadn't seen there before, it's tucked right at the back behind the tree trunk, it's from Chris to me, and I thought we had agreed not to buy each other presents this year as we had spent too much on the house. Mum nudges dad and looks just as excited as I am to open it, I'm momentarily confused as I try to read what it is, he's bought us a voucher for a whole weekend at a spa in January, treatments, dinner, everything. It's so thoughtful, it's just what we need, I'm about to ask who will look after the children when I see my mum pulling her diary out from its hiding place underneath the sofa.

Once all of the presents are unwrapped I try to collect up the piles of discarded paper and make a pathway through the room. Jasmine is obsessed with dolls and now has a few more to add to her collection, complete with clothes, a bath, and a travel system. Harrison is dinosaur mad and is arranging his new additions in a very neat row running the length of the room. He also has a giant stuffed dinosaur, dinosaur pyjamas, and a set of dinosaur jigsaw puzzles.

My mum and I leave Chris and my dad with a tool set to remove the toys from their packaging, it's not an easy job. We sort the rubbish and go to make a start in the kitchen. The turkey is roasting nicely in the oven so we spend a bit of time making the table look nice. Mum has added some greenery to Harrison's table decoration from a few days earlier. I've made the Christmas crackers and filled them with little gifts that I've been collecting throughout the year. Jasmine has a little pink beaded bracelet with a J on it. I've given my mum a pair of earrings she admired in a shop window a few months ago, Dad has got a silver keychain of a boat that I thought he would like. I found Harrison a squidgy toy that you are supposed to throw at the wall and watch it walk back down, I'm not sure if it will work but it should be fun for him to try. Chris has got chocolate sprouts in his and I've filled my own with my favourite hand cream.

I ask my mum if she would mind keeping an eye on the lunch while I have a quick shower, she tells me that of course she doesn't mind, I'm to take my time and leave it all to her. I'm about to tell her there really isn't very much to do but I don't want to spoil her fun.

The hot water is massaging my shoulders and as I rub the shampoo into my hair my mind starts to wander. I can see a little boy, he looks quite a lot like Harrison but I know it isn't him, I can see the boy who I know now is Callum so vibrantly, the sun is shining on his hair, making it look like pure gold. I can see him running around the field in his little denim shorts chasing his football. Then the ball rolls down the hill nearing the river, he runs after it but he can't keep up with it, the ball rolls into the river, so Callum follows, the river isn't too deep, we've played in it before, but today it is windy, the tree tops are swaying, the speed of the wind means it whistles through the branches. Suddenly the ball starts to disappear from view, and as I scream his name and run into the river after him Callum disappears under the water.

I towel myself dry while I am trying to make sense of what I've just seen, how can an imaginary friend evoke such strong feelings. I make a promise to myself to see a doctor when Christmas is all over, but for now I try my hardest to lock Callum away in a box in my brain, back where he came from. I get dressed and dry my hair, then I dab some concealer around my eyes to try to make myself look less tired, that spa weekend is just what I need. With a spritz of perfume and a last brush through my hair I take a deep breath and I'm ready. I'm determined to leave the past firmly in its place, at least for the next few days. I have a hungry family to feed.

I'm wearing my favourite comfy clothes paired with the necklace my mum and dad gave me this morning, it's a beautiful silver butterfly on a long chain, I've always loved butterflies, I remember chasing them around the park when I was little, I think I even had a book so I could identify them.

Despite not doing much this morning we are all ravenous, the roast potatoes are extra crispy on the outside and light and fluffy on the inside, the turkey is a lovely deep bronze colour and my mum's home grown vegetables are perfect. The children even eat the sprouts that nanny grew.

"Lucy, my darling girl, that was simply amazing, thank you very much."

"Thanks Dad, I'm glad you enjoyed it, there's Christmas pudding too, but shall we walk Lupo in a bit and then have the pudding when we get back?"

"Good plan." Say Chris and my mum together.

The snow has stopped falling but there is still a fresh covering on the ground making everything look clean and new. We wander around the park delighting in making new footprints in the virgin snow, the children are taking in turns to throw a stick for Lupo.

"Mummy, why don't we take Lupo to the river? Daddy takes us there with him."

"No!" I don't mean to sound so sharp but I can't go near the river. Open water terrifies me, it always has done. Given how much my parents love the water it makes no sense but that's just how it is. Jasmine looks as though she's about to cry, I must have scared her, the others know about my fear and know now not to mention it, they've given up hope of ever getting me near the water.

I tell Jasmine gently that we can't go to the river or I won't be able to push her on a swing, she loves the swings and she's running off in their direction, calling back over her shoulder for me to race her there.

As I'm pushing her skywards I start to think about the river thing. I don't like the sea but I'd rather be near the sea than a river. I remember early on in our relationship Chris thought he was being incredibly romantic by arranging a surprise day out for us. I was horrified when we arrived at a car park advertising rowing boats for hire. I tried to make excuses to leave, to go anywhere but there. He had thought I was telling him in a roundabout way that I wasn't interested in him so I had to confess my fear of the river to him. He didn't laugh as I had thought he might, he held my hand and said it was a good thing, because up until that point he'd thought I was too perfect to be real. So we'd gone for a walk through the countryside instead and had a fantastic day, eating our picnic on dry land rather than in a boat.

Harrison is looking tired from running around and throwing endless sticks for Lupo and its turning cold. As we walk home the sky once again dusts us with an array of shimmering flakes, Harrison is trying to catch them in his hand. Once we are home we are ready to sit down to have our Christmas pudding and another glass of wine. Dad pours brandy over the pudding and sets fire to it, just like he always does. When we are finished Jasmine asks if she can watch her new film, we all agree that a film would be a perfect idea.

"Come on Harrison, let's go and watch this with your sister." Says my dad, although I think he would rather watch anything else but her chosen Disney movie.

"That's his excuse for a snooze on the sofa." Says my mum with a knowing wink.

I suggest she goes for a sit down too but I catch her looking at the pile of used crockery, I know what she's thinking so I assure her that Chris can help me to load the dish washer, and there's not much else to do. She agrees that a sit down might be nice but makes me promise to call her if I need any help.

Sophie

Despite Jacks failure to be here with us the lunch is a great success, Carrie tells me that I am a brilliant cook, she only wishes Jack could cook something other than beans on toast. Josh laughs and says he could never cook much either until recently, I didn't think he had improved at all but I keep that to myself. I really am starting to worry about Jack because he should have been here hours ago now. I notice a worried Carrie keeps checking the time too. I tell her that he never shows up on time on Christmas day, last year he was a whole day late! But I'm honestly getting increasingly worried too.

Josh groans and rubs his slightly rounded tummy, he says it was a lovely lunch but he couldn't possibly eat another thing for hours. I know that's a lie, within the next half an hour he will be unwrapping the Quality Street chocolates and eating all the purple ones before anyone else can get to them.

Daisy asks Auntie Carrie if she can show her the new princess doll she got from her grandparents this morning. Carrie tells her of course she can, she would love to see her, then she holds out her hand and says "Lead the way princess Daisy." I think again how lovely she is, and wonder what Jack is playing at.

I tell my parents to go through to the lounge and I'll bring them some coffee in a moment. Josh doesn't need telling twice, any excuse to avoid the tidying up and he's gone, probably to make a start on those chocolates. He follows my mum and dad from the room and I catch him yawning, hopefully he will stay awake and chat to them for a bit while I get the kitchen straight.

I try calling Jack again but have to leave yet another message. "Jack, where the hell are you? We've just finished eating, Carrie is here as well and she's wondering where you are. If you are still in bed hung over I promise you I will make your life miserable for the foreseeable future, if you are on your way hurry up please, but drive safely. Bye."

Hanging up the phone I'm feeling uneasy, it's true that Jack has often been unreliable but he knew Carrie was coming here today, I can't honestly believe he would stand her up too. Something doesn't feel right.

Lucy

As the credits begin to roll I wake up, I'm sure Chris looks like he's just woken up too. My dad is still asleep, he is hiding his eyes behind his paper hat that came out of his cracker, only his rumbling snores give him away.

"Grandad, wake up! You missed the end of the film; you didn't see him turn into a prince."

"Never mind Jasmine, I'm sure we'll watch it again another time."

I'm sure my dad is rolling his eyes as he says that.

"Okay Grandddad, I'll let you watch it again tomorrow," She's addressing her Grandad with her serious face. "But now that you've all had a sleep it's time to play games."

So for the next few hours we play board games, some of which make no sense but the children are happy. We eat far too many chocolates and finish another bottle of wine. The afternoon soon merges into the evening. It's becoming dark outside but the logs are crackling on the fire so we are all warm and cosy. I've managed to check my phone a few times but there's nothing from any of the hospitals, I'm thinking that maybe I should widen my search area again.

"I'm huggee Mummy." Harrison says after he has won his first game of the afternoon.

I unwind my legs from under me and get up from the floor, I stretch out the kinks in my muscles and I tell him to give me five minutes to get a few bits out to eat. Dad says he really doesn't think he could eat anything else. I tell him not to worry, I'm not doing much food, just some crackers and cheese, there's a Christmas cake too I say with a wicked grin because I know my dad can never resist a piece of Christmas cake. My mum was up out of her chair at the mention of cheese!

Another cheese board is demolished between us and washed down with another bottle of wine, we are all feeling very sleepy now. Harrison has managed to eat half a pack of grapes and a large slice of cake; he is now struggling to keep his eyes open. I scoop him up just as he closes his eyes and I carry him up to bed. He can have a bath and clean his teeth in the morning, right now he just needs his bed, I carefully slide him under his duvet and stroke his hair as he goes to sleep. I lay down with him for a moment snuggled up to his warm little body. It's tempting to stay here and close my eyes too but I've got parents to look after, so I kiss him softly then I quietly close his door. I pass Chris on the landing with Jasmine in his arms, she is almost asleep too so he slides her into bed, carefully arranging her stuffed animals to their special bedtime places before creeping out of her room.

We go back down to find my parents have tidied everything away and my mum is making a pot of tea. Dad is throwing another log onto the fire and Lupo wiggles closer to the warmth. We sit quietly for a few minutes, enjoying the warmth from the fire and relaxing in the peace and quiet.

"Mum, Dad, do you remember where we were one summer when I lost my new ball in the river? It's been on my mind all afternoon, I feel like it is an important memory although I can't explain why."

"I really don't know love." Says my mum, she looks totally blank. "Do you remember Charlie?"

He is shaking his head and he says he doesn't ever remember me losing a ball in a river, they say that they wouldn't have let me play near a river on my own, but I never even wanted to go near a river for starters so he is pretty sure it could never have happened. I feel like Callum is in the room with me now, he feels so real when I talk about him.

This is crazy, how can they not remember this day, I can feel my frustration bubbling over "But I remember it, it came to me earlier after I realised Callum was my imaginary friend, I was in a field with him, he chased my new ball and then it got swept away by the water and he disappeared under the water too, although you obviously wouldn't have seen that bit." I hadn't noticed but during my outburst I'm standing up, I'm shouting quite loudly too.

Mum tells me she's sorry but my dad is right, they never let me play alone anywhere when I was little, especially not near any water, and I wouldn't have gone near a river anyway because I've always been scared. She really doesn't remember this ever happening.

But I know it did happen; my memories of this are crystal clear. I want to scream at them, this is so important to me so why can't they remember? I sink back onto my chair and think about it again, I know I'm right.

"Mum, Dad, I know it really did happen. It was summertime and I can clearly see us playing in a meadow, there were daisies and buttercups growing everywhere. Callum was chasing a ball and they both went into the water. I can see it all so clearly."

Mum tells me that maybe I had a dream about one of my adventures with my pretend friend; maybe that's what has happened. I know that my mum means well with what she's saying but I know she is wrong. I'm sure it happened and I'm sure that's why I don't like the water. I can see Chris is about to say something too and I don't want our day to be spoilt so I quickly suggest a brandy before bedtime, which as I'd predicted it diffuses any further conversations about my state of mind, although I'm quietly frustrated that they aren't helping me to piece this mystery together.

Sophie

Daisy is sleeping peacefully after a long day filled with excitement and too much chocolate. My parents went home a while ago, they were a bit annoyed that they hadn't seen Jack but despite what they seem to think it wasn't my fault, my mum had checked three times that I had remembered to invite him. Josh has now poured Carrie and I a glass of wine, he takes a whisky through to the lounge with him to watch a film and leaves us talking in the kitchen. Carrie is understandably very upset that Jack hasn't turned up, or even phoned her. I wonder if she feels a bit awkward being in our house without him so I reassure her the best I can that she's very welcome here.

"Thank you for having me here today, it's been lovely spending time with you all, Daisy is adorable." But then she looks uncomfortable as she says "I've been thinking, do you think Jack has changed his mind about me? I keep thinking maybe that's why he has stayed away today."

I don't even need to think about that, I tell her "There's no way that's the case. Firstly, he promised me he would be here, secondly he promised you that he'd be here, thirdly....well I'm not sure but I know he is really happy with you, something must have happened."

"So where is he?" Is her quiet reply. I'm not sure she even expects me to answer. I think for a bit and then I ask her if she can contact any of his friends and find out if they've seen him, she shakes her head and tells me although they sometimes meet up with his friends for a drink she doesn't know any of them very well. I don't anymore either. But then I have an idea, what about Bea who lives in the flat above him, I think I have her as a facebook friend, I can see if I can get her to go and bang on his door. Carrie agrees that it makes sense, it's a good idea, and probably the only option we have left aside from one of us making a long drive ourselves in the ice and snow.

As I'm typing out the message to Bea on my phone I get some nibbles out from the fridge, not because either of us is hungry but because it gives me something productive to do.

It doesn't take long for Bea to send us her reply; it says she has been down to Jacks flat and banged on the door. She said there was no answer and it sounded quiet in there with no lights on, so, I know

Jack will probably be furious with me but I tell her where his spare key is hidden and ask her to go in. She's a bit unsure about doing so but after I explain the situation to her she agrees.

Carrie is nibbling on cheese while we wait to hear back from Bea and I'm refilling my wine glass, we are both finding it hard to sit still. Just a short while later Bea reports that she's been into Jacks flat, there's no sign of him but his mobile phone is plugged in and sitting on the table, an alarm is gently vibrating and flashing up a reminder saying "*time to go to Sophie's*" So, that explains why he isn't answering his calls, but even more worryingly, it shows us he was definitely planning to come today, so where is he?

We agree that we need to call the police. Carrie asks me to make the call, her hands are shaking and there's a quiver in her voice. I think about what I need to say and then I make the call, I explain to the officer what has happened but they say that unfortunately because he's a grown man who actually hasn't been missing for very long there isn't really much they can do about it. I leave mine and Carries numbers as well as my landline number and hang up feeling exhausted. I'm trying to tell myself he's hung-over and sleeping it off on the sofa at a friend's house somewhere, but deep down I don't quite believe it, something feels wrong.

Because I don't really know what else to do with her I suggest Carrie goes up for a soak in the bath, I promise her I'll let her know straight away if I hear from Jack, she reluctantly agrees and hugs me as she leaves the room. I go in search of Josh to update him, he doesn't say much, just "Okay, that's all you can do." Which is pretty much what I thought he'd say. He moves up to make room for me on the sofa and gives me a reassuring hug. Pluto the cat joins us too, squashing her silky body in between us and purring loudly without a care in the world.

Hospital

It's almost midnight on Christmas day when Betsy does the last ward round of her shift; it's been a long day working on a skeleton staff. She doesn't mind working today even though it's Christmas day, her children have grown up and they have to divide their time between her and their in laws. She had hosted their own version of Christmas together last weekend. She's checking all the equipment and updating the notes on the man they have named Mr Christmas, just until they find out who he is. She carefully smoothes his covers and just as she turns to leave she's sure he twitches his hand, so she watches him for a few more minutes, happy just sitting by his bedside lost in her own thoughts, he's the last patient she needs to check on tonight and she has no reason to rush home. Then a moment later she smiles as he slowly opens his eyes.

Chapter 9 Celeste age Celeste age 8

I keep asking my daddy where my mummy is, the teacher at school said I need to ask mummy to wash my school uniform, she has said this lots of times now, she was talking to another lady in my classroom and I think they were talking about me, they kept looking over at me, I didn't like it. When I got home from school I asked daddy where my mummy was, I keep asking him but he won't tell me, he just gets cross and tells me to shut up, and then he drinks lots of drinks and takes his special medicine with the needle. I got myself some dinner again tonight, I can spread jam onto the bread and cut the crusts off all by myself and sometimes there is milk in the fridge to go with it.

The teachers at school let me have a cooked lunch in the big hall now, they got cross with me when I kept leaving my lunch box at home, I told them that I hadn't forgotten it, I just didn't see why I should bring it with me to school when there wasn't anything in it. The food at school changes every day, they have chips on a Friday which is nice, they have other foods on different days but I don't know what everything is, they have lots of foods I haven't seen before. There is a roast chicken but it doesn't look much like a chicken, there are lots of green things that the ladies say I should try. It's really nice to eat something hot before we have to go outside to play, if it is a really cold day I ask the ladies for some extra food and then I eat as slowly as I can so that I can stay inside for a bit longer, I don't like playing outside in the cold because my cardigan doesn't keep me very warm. The lady on the playground tells me I should have a coat.

That night I do my homework and then I ask daddy if he wants any bread with jam on but he tells me to be quiet and to go to my room. I spend a lot of time in my room but there isn't much to do in there, I practise my spellings that the teacher gave me at school a few days ago, I think the spelling test is tomorrow, then I read the book that I am allowed to bring home from school. I wish I had a TV or some more books. Once I asked my daddy if I could have some books to read or some paper and pencils but he laughed and told me to dream on.

Chapter 10   Sophie

It's early when I wake, although I'm not sure wake really is the right word, I know I slept a few hours fitfully on and off all night, I automatically woke every hour to check my phone, I'm caught in that place between being asleep and being fully alert. There's little point trying to sleep anymore now so I pull on yesterday's clothes and creep downstairs. I'm not at all surprised to find Carrie already sitting at the kitchen table cradling a cup of tea.

"I hope you don't mind me helping myself?"

"Of course I don't mind, did you manage to sleep?"

"Did you?" Asks Carrie, mirroring my concern.

I make myself a coffee and fill the toaster before sitting down opposite her. We both jump as my phone buzzes with a message. It was just Bea offering to go and check Jacks flat again if we wanted her to, we reply yes please and then we sit staring at my phone waiting for her to reply, I butter the toast that neither of us really wants but we eat for something to do. When my phone buzzes again I read the message and shake my head, Carrie seems to know what I mean as she answers with a sad smile and crumbles her toast crust between her fingers.

We pass the morning together while Josh takes Daisy off to his parent's house, we were all supposed to be spending the day there today, I promise to join him as soon as I can. He kisses me goodbye and I promise to call him as soon as I hear anything from Jack. The house feels extra quiet with the two of them gone, Carrie and I continue to sit together in silence, we are making endless cups of tea and wrapping our hands around the warmth, each of us lost in our own thoughts.

I'm remembering back to when I was little, my mum always said Jack's name was Jackson, she would get cross if I called him Jack, but then we started to call him Jack all the time as he grew up. I remember him being really annoying as all little brothers are, then as he grew up he became quieter for a while, he livened up again when he went to high school and evolved entirely when he went to university. We always got along pretty well for siblings, it's odd how neither of us are very close to our mum or dad, we don't seem to have much in common with them, Jack and I are always up for an adventure where as they are content hidden away on their farm with just each other for company. It's quite sweet really that they have been together for all of these years and still appear to be happy together, not many people are lucky enough to have that these days.

Carrie's brain is trying to process her situation; she isn't sure if she is angry or worried, where is Jack? And why isn't he with her where he is supposed to be? She was looking forward to their first Christmas together as a proper couple. They'd met at the beginning of December last year so it was too early on in their relationship to spend Christmas together that year, one day though, if she's brave enough, she'll confess to Sophie it was partly her fault he was late getting to hers last year, although it wasn't her fault he'd met up with friends after she'd left his house Christmas morning resulting in him being so late. She also keeps checking his special present is safely tucked away in her bag. If their relationship is over she's no idea what she'll do.

It is late in the afternoon now, the daylight is gradually fading into dusk and it's becoming colder again. Carrie and I have spent the afternoon together looking through old photo albums. I don't have any of Jack and me as young children, I'll have to remember to ask mum and dad if I can have some of theirs to make a copy of. There's a good one here of Jack about age eleven, he is dressed in an ill fitting suit but he still manages to look handsome, his hair is so blonde it is almost white as he stands in the sun, his hands are in his pockets and he is striking a cheeky pose. We were off to church that day although I don't remember the reason why, it wasn't something we did very often. I had just had my twelfth birthday and I had been given my first camera, I had carried it everywhere with me back then, I had it on a red chord around my neck, I was convinced I was going to grow up to be a photographer. I'm not sure when I gave up on that dream, or really why I became a legal secretary, I suppose real life kicked in nudging the dreams of photography aside.

We've got so used to the silence that when my phone suddenly rings it takes us both by surprise, I hold my breath as I answer it, putting it on speaker mode for Carrie in case its news from Jack, we listen carefully as we are told by a nurse that Jackson was in an accident and is recovering in hospital, he matches the description given to the police by us, his medical records also confirm the identification. The nurse tells us to come in to see him in the morning as he is very tired, too tired for visitors tonight, she wants to talk to us tomorrow before we see him. I thank her for calling but it feels a bit surreal, I should have asked to talk to him now, to put our minds at rest that he is alright. It was just such a relief to know that he was safe I forgot to ask any questions.

We are obviously both relieved to hear he is alive and being looked after, but why does she need to talk to us before we see him? He must have sustained a terrible injury of some kind that she doesn't want to explain over the phone. We imagine all sorts of possible scenarios, none of them are good.

Resigned to the fact that there's nothing more we can do tonight I leave Carrie with a terrible TV movie and a turkey sandwich while I go to meet up with Josh and Daisy, I won't be able to stay at my in-laws for very long but I know they'll understand, Josh has told them Jack was missing. They are quite fond of Jack, most people are when they meet him, he has a charm about him that is impossible not to fall for.

Hospital

"Hello there Mr Christmas, how are you feeling?"

I've just opened my eyes and everything looks unfamiliar, this isn't my home, everything looks too white, and much too tidy. I tell the lady that I'm okay, and then I look again at my surroundings and ask her what's going on. She tells me that I am in hospital, I was bought in very late on Christmas Eve, I had been hit by a car and was found unconscious by the side of the road. I wasn't expecting to hear that but it explains why every inch of my body is hurting.

She tells me that I have broken my left leg and I have got fractured ribs on both sides, then she adjusts my sling and says I have also broken my left arm, and I have quite a bump to the head. I put a hand to my head and feel a large bandage across my forehead, I think it's wrapped around my head, subconsciously I rub my forehead as I try to think about what happened, did she say I was unconscious? I ask her about that and she says that I was unresponsive for almost twenty-four hours. Whoever hit me did a good job of it and the police are still looking into what happened, they have launched an appeal for witnesses. A group of people on their way home from a party found me in the road and called for an ambulance.

"Where was I?" I manage to ask her, it's hurting to think, and to breathe.

She says that she hasn't got those details here in the file, but now that I am awake the police will have some questions for me. Because I didn't have a phone or any identification on me when I came in she wants to take some personal details if I feel up to it, I nod my agreement then ask her for a glass of water, my throat feels like sandpaper.

She rushes off to get a fresh jug of water for me and says the doctor might want a quick look at me too before she starts questioning me. I can only manage to say "Okay nurse."

"Molly," She says with a smile "My name is Molly, and who are you just so I can update your chart? We can't keep calling you Mr Christmas."

"Nice to meet you Molly, I'm Callum." I tell her. Then I close my eyes and fall back against the welcoming softness of the pillows.

Lucy

We all sleep in later this morning. The children were tired because of all the usual Christmas excitement, my parents are used to lying in now they are retired and Chris never wakes up before nine o'clock unless he absolutely has too. I slept in for a different reason entirely, as soon as I was sure everyone else was fast asleep last night I sat up with a pot of tea and phoned around as many hospitals as I could before exhaustion took over and sent me to bed. In between phone calls I tried internet searches for Callum but it was pointless without any further information to go on. I also searched for information on hallucinations but I didn't I like what I was reading, deep down I honestly believe he is, or was real.

I decide that as nobody else is getting up I'll take advantage of it and stay in bed too. As I close my eyes and snuggle back down under the duvet, rolling over to wrap myself in its warmth, I'm reminded of rolling down a hill somewhere, Callum is beside me and we are giggling as the prickly grass scratches our legs as we are gaining speed and tumbling further down the grassy hill. There are a couple of people waiting for us at the bottom of the hill and I think one of them is my mum, she looks young and happy. I'm not sure who she is with, maybe it's my dad, although I have no memories of him at all. Behind them I can see the river, and then I can hear myself calling out to them "Mumma we're coming."

I've frozen in time again in a world that has stopped moving, it's all making sense now, the world as I know it has shifted once again but it's all so clear now, the pieces of the puzzle are coming together at last. Callum is my brother, and I can remember my real mother. Scarier still, I know with absolute certainty that my brother went into the water and didn't ever come out again. I don't remember anything else until my 'parents' took me home with them. I remember a photo from that first day with my new parents, I was wearing a new woolly hat with a pink bobble on it so it must have been winter by then, that means I've still mislaid a whole chunk of time, I wonder what exactly happened to my mother, and my brother, hopefully it will all come back to me, a fragment at a time, just as the other memories have.

My brain is working overtime trying to unravel and piece together my shattered memories. Then I realise that if Callum died it must have been recorded, therefore, I should be able to trace him, I'm sure I can. I go down to find my laptop, wrapping myself in a cardigan that I've left lying around in the kitchen, my pyjamas are thin and I'm shivering. If I was three when I was adopted I can roughly work out the year Callum died, so I type it into the internet search and wait. There are pages of links to follow, I start to scroll down through the pages clicking on anything that might be relevant, quickly dismissing it if it isn't. I've drunk two cups of coffee and I'm almost at the end of the search results when I find it. The dates don't match what I was looking for but without a shadow of a doubt I know I have found him.

16.9.1988   **Drowned.**

In a tragic accident late yesterday afternoon the body of a little boy was swept away in the river North. Extensive searches were carried out almost immediately but he wasn't found. The current was exceptionally strong at that time and it is feared his body followed the flow of the river and may have been taken out to sea. The details are still patchy but he is thought to be a young boy called Callum White aged 4. Searches are due to have resumed at first light this morning.

I can barely breathe, in a matter of seconds I've discovered I had a brother, and that tragically he died. I read it again, slower this time. I am desperately trying to remember anything else that's been buried in my head. I want to bang my head in frustration because there are no further memories surfacing, but there is a link to another story that I click on with my shaking hands.

17.9.1988 **2 people killed, head on collision.**

In the early hours of yesterday morning emergency services were called to a RTA involving a campervan. The two adults were killed on impact with a tree. A little girl was found sitting on the verge nearby, she had cuts and bruises and it is thought she was involved in the accident but managed to escape unharmed. She bears a striking resemblance to the description given of the missing boy who is presumed drowned in the area. The girl was clearly in shock and is being looked after by social services. There is still no news of the missing boy.

It's my life. It's my life that I had intentionally or not blocked out. Without really knowing what I'm doing next I am sending the articles to print, I feel the need to keep them. I can hear movement coming from upstairs now, I'm not sure who it is that's up but I can't cope with any of this, it's just too much. I grab my car keys and leave.

"Daddy, wake up, where's Mummy? It's breakfast time, Daddy, wake up!"

"Morning guys, what's all the noise for?" Chris says still blurry from sleep.

"Daddy, we are totally starving."

Chris opens his eyes to see Jasmine and Harrison standing next to the bed, Jasmine has obviously taken charge because Harrison is just nodding along next to his big sister.

"Okay, let's go and find Mum."

"But Daddy, you can't, Mummy isn't here, I've looked everywhere in the whole house."

"Well she has probably taken Lupo for a walk."

"No Daddy, Lupo is still here."

"Come on then you two." He says scooping them up and putting one under each arm, making them laugh. They meet Charlie on the landing and all go down together. Chris can't smell coffee which is odd, Lucy always brews a big pot when she gets up, and Lupo desperately wants to go out, something isn't right.

"Ann, are you okay love?" Charlie asks his wife, she is sitting incredibly still at the kitchen table and she is clutching a pile of papers, she silently shakes her head and hands Charlie the sheets of paper. Chris senses the mood and ushers the children through to the living room to watch TV with a biscuit while he makes them a real breakfast.

"What's happened?" He asks coming back in to the room. "Where's Lucy?"

Charlie hands him the stack of papers, he reads them silently then sits back in his chair, a look of bewilderment on his face.

They are all silent for a while then Ann takes charge of the children's breakfast, she makes them a plate of boiled egg and soldiers each with a cup of fresh juice.

"I'll sit with the children while they eat this then we'll try to work out where Lucy is and what's going on." And she tries her hardest to give them a reassuring smile as she leaves the room.

"I just don't get it Charlie; does Lucy think she had a brother that died? It might not be connected at all, and there is no proof. Or does she think this is her imaginary friend? It's all such a mess."

"I agree son. I can't just sit here though, I'm tying my brain into knots, can I walk the dog?"

"Okay, why not, I'll call you when Lucy gets back."

"Let me take the children too, it will do them good to run around in the fresh air, it gives rain later so I'll get them out while I can."

"Good idea. I'll try calling Lucy again then I'll get the children ready."

But as he does he realises her phone is laying on the worktop, and its flat, he plugs it into charge ready for her when she gets back home.

I don't know where I'm going, I'm driving aimlessly with no destination in mind, but luckily the petrol tank is almost full. I just needed to escape the confines of the house, I needed to be able to think and breathe. I felt like I was drowning in a pool of emotions. I think I've been gone for almost an hour when I see a sign for a nature reserve which seems like a good place to stop and stretch my legs. The sky is darkening to an inky shade of deep blue and the air is bitterly cold, I pull my cardigan tighter around my body as I get out of the car and I begin to follow the footpath that takes me deep into the towering trees.

I'm bought to a sudden halt when I see a massive lake ahead of me. I'm frozen to the spot initially but slowly I begin to edge forwards, my feet are slowly closing the distance between myself and the murky water, my fear of water is temporarily forgotten, all rational thoughts have been left behind.

I'm only inches away from the edge now because somehow my fear has made me stronger today. I desperately need answers. As I look down into the depths of the water I'm remembering Callum on that last day again, he didn't want to lose his ball so he went after it, he tried to grab onto the trees and the roots on river bank, I could see him being dragged further away but I couldn't get to him, I can hear myself screaming his name and then I can see myself in the water too, then I'm being rescued by a boy, he must have been about fifteen or sixteen, he dragged me out of the water even though I fought him, he didn't understand what was happening. I don't know who he was, where were my parents? So many unanswered questions plague my mind but all I can do is to stare into the water and take my mind back through time, I'm willing myself to remember.

"Are you alright Miss? You are awfully close the edge."

I thought I was alone but an elderly man is standing next to me, he is dressed head to toe in bright orange hiking gear, I've got no idea where he came from or how long he has been there, he has a tiny white dog sitting patiently at his feet.

"I'm fine, thank you." I say, and I try to smile at him.

"Forgive me for saying this Miss but you really don't look fine at all."

"No, I probably don't, but I will be, thank you. I think I'll go home now."

"Good idea Miss, I can feel a storm coming."

I think he might be right about the storm; I thank him for his kindness and make a fuss of his dog before I make my way back. The narrow pathway winds its way through the trees and takes me back to my car, it's time to go home and face up to what I've discovered.

Despite it still only being late morning the sky is almost black by the time I arrive home. As I pull onto the driveway the heavens finally unleash the torrential rain that has been filling the clouds all morning, the sky is temporarily lit up by a bolt of lightning exploding above me and I make it inside the house just a clap of thunder rumbles and shakes the ground beneath me.

"Mummy, Mummy, where have you been?" Jasmine launches herself at me the minute I walk in the door. The others are only seconds behind her, I feel bad for worrying them all, but I really don't feel like talking it all over.

I draw upon my rehearsed lie and tell them that I went out to the shops to have a look at the sales, but there wasn't anything we needed so I came home. Only the children believe this lie though because clearly I haven't been shopping, I don't have a bag or even a purse with me.

"I'll get started on lunch shall I? What does everyone fancy?" I say because they are all looking at me, I feel uncomfortable and I want to turn around and leave again.

"Chocolate!" Chime the children, so I tell them they can each have something out of their selection boxes while I am cooking. My mum frowns at me and leaves, beckoning me to follow.

Dad and Chris are waiting for us in the kitchen, I can see that my mum has already made a saucepan of turkey soup for lunch and another loaf of bread is rising. Chris puts the newspaper articles and a cup of coffee down in front of me, I'd forgotten I'd left them out in plain view, although knowing they've all read the articles means I don't have to tell them anything that they won't already know.

"Lucy love, your Mum and I didn't know about any of this. We told you everything we knew about your old life."

"I know Dad, and I know it's not your fault. But at least I know now that Callum was real, he was my brother." And now that I'm saying it out loud I can't hold back the tears any longer, I've gained and lost a brother in such a short space of time, when did life become so cruel?

My mum is about to say something but she's cut off by my phone ringing, Chris passes it to me but I don't have the energy, I pass it back and ask him to answer it, or to turn it off.

He answers it and I listen while he says "Hello, Lucy's phone, Umm, yes, that sounds about right, oh, really, are you sure, well okay then, you'd better give me the address." Then he reaches for a pen and scribbles something down before thanking them and ending the call. He puts the phone back down then paces around the kitchen absently scratching his head before coming back to sit in front of me.

"Okay, are you ready for this?" Chris says looking directly at me.

"Why? What is it? Nothing could make my day any worse."

"Well, I'm not sure how to say this but that was Molly."

"I don't know anyone called Molly." I jump in before he can say anymore; I'm too tired for this.

"Let me finish, Molly is a nurse, you spoke to her a few days ago."

As he is talking I'm holding my breath, I can remember Molly now so I just nod as he carries on talking.

"She said you left her your number, you were looking for Callum."

"I know, it was crazy, we know he's gone now though so let's just forget all about it and try to move on can we?"

"Well, it might not be that easy, the reason she was phoning just now was to tell you that she thinks she's found him, he matches the description you gave and he has regained consciousness now. His memory is still very hazy but he said he is called Callum."

I'm speechless, mum and dad are sitting silently open mouthed too.

"But how can this be? Now that I know that my brother died it can't be my Callum, but if so, who did I see in the hospital?" I'm not sure who I'm asking my questions to, nobody can give me the answers I need, my family are all clearly as confused as I am.

"Lucy, I can't answer any of those questions but the one person who might be able to help you is in a hospital a few hours away, so I suggest we have lunch, take a bit of time to process this news this afternoon and go to see him tomorrow."

What does he mean, go and see him tomorrow. We have to go today, I have to see him, we have to sort this mess out. I'm shaking my head insisting we go to the hospital now. Then my mum puts her arms on my shoulders and makes me take a deep breath to steady myself. After a moment I'm calmer and I slump back into my seat.

"Lucy love, Chris is right, you need to eat and sleep, you need to get yourself together." Mum says while she is taking the bread out of the oven, it smells delicious.

"I'm fine Mum." I say, then as I stand up to refill my coffee cup I see my reflection mirrored in the French windows and I see what they can all see. I am a mess, my hair hasn't been brushed and I look exhausted, I've even been out walking through the woods in my pyjamas and slippers so no wonder that poor old man was so concerned about me, I look unwell, like I've wandered straight out of a hospital ward.

"Okay," I reluctantly agree "We'll go first thing tomorrow, will you be able to look after the children please?"

"You know we will."

"Thanks Mum. Now how about we have lunch while that bread is still warm?"

So as the day continues we spend a relaxing afternoon together, we play games with the children and carry on like we are a normal family. None of us voice any of the thousands of questions we each have, there's just no point. During the afternoon the children have a snooze so I take the opportunity to go for a soak in the bath, my muscles are aching from being out in the cold this morning, or maybe they ache from lack of sleep, or maybe the deep aching comes from the battering my life seems to have taken recently.

There is still leftover Turkey so for dinner that evening Chris turns it into a curry because curries are the only thing that he can cook, then although not exactly culinary correct we follow the curry with cheese and crackers. I tell Jasmine and Harrison they can stay up extra late tonight if they get ready for bed now, so they eagerly rush up the stairs. Chris offers to take charge of their bath time while I tidy up. Mum and dad have taken Lupo for a quick walk.

The house falls silent for a moment until I hear giggling from upstairs in the bathroom, normally I enjoy a few minutes alone but not tonight. I go and help Harrison into his pyjamas and dressing gown, and then he helps me to make the popcorn. I explain to them both that I have to go and visit a friend in the morning, I tell them that daddy will be coming too and that their nana and grandad will be looking after them. They are both happy with that once Jasmine has checked to see if my mum will make them her special boiled eggs for breakfast, I assure her that she will although I have no idea what makes them special boiled eggs.

As soon as my mum and dad are back from their walk we all settle down in front of a Christmas movie and munch on popcorn and chocolates, I make a vow to myself to be healthier in the new year.

Chapter 11 Celeste age 8 ½

Today my teacher said there was a lady here to see me, I told her that I didn't know any ladies and she laughed and said this as a special lady from social services, she just wanted to have a chat to me. We went into a room in the school that I haven't seen before; it was a nicer room than my classroom because there were squishy chairs and beanbags. The lady told me she was called Linda, she asked me questions about who looked after me at home. I told her I was grown up and looked after myself. She asked about my mummy and daddy so I told her that my mummy has gone somewhere, I hadn't seen her for a while. I told her that my daddy wasn't very well so he slept on the sofa quite a lot and he always took his special medicine, she didn't know what the special medicine was so I told her that his friends always bought it to our flat for him and he put it in his body with the special needle that I was never allowed to touch. Then I told her that once I did touch it, it was my mummy's medicine though and mummy had fallen asleep with the special needle still hanging out of her arm so I carefully took it out and put it on the floor beside her. I think it was the next day that I stopped seeing my mummy, she was gone when I got home from school and she never came back.

Linda wrote lots of words in her notebook, I can read quite well but her book was upside down so I couldn't see what she was writing. Linda was nice to me, she said I was clever and I noticed that she smelled nice, I wonder if that's what roses smell like.

After Linda had gone I went back to my classroom and it was time for lunch, today I tried something called steamed pudding, it was so nice, and it came with a sauce on top of it called custard, I would like to have custard on top of everything.

When lunch had finished I was walking back to my classroom when Linda found me again, she took me back to the room and told me that she had looked for my mummy, this made me happy because I miss my mummy a lot. Linda told me that she had some very sad news for me. She looked very serious and said that my mummy was in heaven, I told her that my grandma was there too. She asked if I knew what heaven was, I shook my head and she explained that heaven is where people go when they die. I know about dying because we had tadpoles in the classroom that died after a boy called Ted put paint in their water.

Then the lady called Linda told me that someone else she works with had been to my house, I asked how she knew where I lived and she didn't answer, she just did a little laugh, I don't know why because I don't think I asked a silly question. Then she told me that I was going to spend a few nights in a house especially for children. I asked her why and she said that because my mummy was in heaven and my daddy wasn't looking after me very well, because of his illness. She said that I could stay in a big house with lots of other children. Then she said that they would give me my breakfast and wash my school uniform and everything. When I asked her if I would still need to do my own bread and jam for tea she shook her head and smiled at me, I think she must have caught a cold because her eyes were suddenly all watery.

I had to go back to my classroom quite soon after that, we were about to start Art, we have lots of different things on the table, some of it looks like rubbish but we have to stick it on our piece of paper to make something called a collage

Chapter 12 Callum

"Sorry Callum, I didn't mean to wake you, I'm Wendy, one of the nurses here, how are you feeling?" she says releasing my arm from the sleeve of the blood pressure machine.

I tell her that I think I'm okay, although I still have a lot of pain in my arm and my head hurts. She says that is to be expected, so she goes to get me some pain relief saying she'll be right back. I thank her although she has already scuttled off. I take a look around the ward; I'm not sure what I'm looking for though. There are five other beds here although only three of them are occupied; everyone else appears to be sleeping.

"Okay Callum, here is your pain relief." Says Wendy, she's back but she's not alone, two police officers are with her and I feel myself panicking. I don't think I've done anything wrong but without my memory it's impossible to say for sure, the police have always made me nervous, I remember hiding from them when I was very young although I don't know where that memory came from, I wonder what I had done, and why are they here now?

Wendy tells me that these police officers have a few questions for me if I feel up to it, she says it with such a kind smile that I don't like to disappoint her, so although I really want to say I'm not feeling up to it I say it is okay.

I sit up and tell them that I can't remember a thing about what happened, I tell them that I have already spoken to another officer about the accident this morning. I really just want them to just go away so I can take my pain relief and go back to sleep. But they tell me that they are here on a slightly different matter, and then he coughs and looks uncomfortable, making me wonder what I might have done.

"Oh, right." I say but I really don't know what they want, Wendy is hovering awkwardly too.

"Well Callum," Says the taller of the two, and he looks at his notebook before carrying on. He says "We've had reports of a missing man matching your description."

I wasn't expecting that but it's a relief to know I must have someone that is missing me, hopefully that means things will start to fall into place now. I realise they are waiting for me to say something so I tell him that is great news. So hopefully that means I have a family who will fill in the blanks, then I ask if that means I can go home now.

The second officer hasn't spoken at all yet and he is looking increasingly uncomfortable, he shifts his weight between his feet whilst avoiding my gaze and he waits for the other officer to speak again. I wonder why he is even here if he isn't going to talk.

"The problem is sir," The officer tells me as he sits down and pulls the chair up closer. I'm starting to get a funny feeling about this. The officer takes a deep breath and looks at his colleague who is once again shifting uncomfortably, then he continues "The person your sister and girlfriend are describing matches you perfectly, right down to the watch you were wearing and the tattoo on your shoulder."

"Okay, that's great but I don't see why that is a problem, just don't tell my girlfriend that I had forgotten her." I joke but neither of them are laughing, Wendy is still smiling kindly at me though.

The policeman clears his throat before telling me "The thing is, we think you are called Jackson, not Callum. Your name is Jackson Hemmingsway."

"No, this is crazy. I'm Callum, Callum something, I can't remember the last bit but my name is definitely Callum."

"Callum, I mean Jack," This is nurse Wendy talking to me now, she looks at me like I'm a little kid "We have looked up Jack Hemmingsway's medical records, we are certain it is you, the scar you have on your abdomen is from when your appendix burst when you were fifteen. We've also checked your blood type and you match Jack Hemmingsway. I'm so sorry; I know this is a lot for you to take in. I have to clock off now but Molly will be taking over from me, you met her yesterday, I'll get her to have a chat with you, okay?"

"Okay" I say although this situation is anything but Okay. "You mentioned my sister, can I call her?"

"You can if you want but it's quite late now, I spoke to her earlier while you were sleeping, I explained what had happened, she will be here first thing in the morning, and your girlfriend is coming with her too I think."

"Right, I think you're right. I need to sleep. I'll see Lucy tomorrow and she will help me make sense of all this."

"Who's Lucy?" Asks Wendy.

"My sister, you said you spoke to Lucy."

"No Jack, your sister is called Sophie, Sophie is coming tomorrow." And she smoothes the bed covers and pats my arm in what I think is supposed to be a reassuring manor and flashes me a last pitying smile as she walks away.

The police tell me they will be in touch with any further developments and then they leave me to rest. It's all too much to process, do I have another sister I'd forgotten about? And maybe I have another girlfriend too? The dull headache I had earlier has turned into a mighty thumping headache now. I lay back against the pillows going over and over everything I've just been told.

I must have fallen asleep because as I open my eyes in the darkness of the ward I can see the faces that created my dreams, there was a little girl that I felt I know but I can't give her a name, then I have a terrible thought as I suddenly wonder if I have a daughter that I have also forgotten about. I try to fall back into the safety of sleep because the world is just too confusing to be part of at the moment.

A while later I sense someone standing next to my bed, part of me is scared that someone to deliver me some more bizarre news so cautiously I open my eyes and I'm relieved when I recognise the face that greets me.

"HI, I'm Molly, I was here when you woke up last night, do you remember me?"

"Yeah, of course I do, is there any chance of some water please?" My throat feels so dry it's hard to swallow.

While she pours me some fresh water she tells me "There's something I should tell you, and I'm really sorry if I did the wrong thing. Please don't get cross but there's a lady been phoning asking if Callum has been bought in," she's got my full attention now so I try to sit up as she says "I didn't know your name when I spoke to her on Christmas Eve but I did take her details as she sounded so worried about you. I really hope you don't mind but I called her back earlier when we thought you were called Callum and she's coming to see you, but now I know your name is Jackson it's confused the situation and I should probably call her back and tell her not to come, what do you think? I know I've messed up and I really am sorry, I thought I was helping."

"Wow, okay," Maybe it's his girlfriend he thinks, but why does he have two names he wonders, "Did she leave her name? You didn't say what her name is."

"Lucy, I'm sorry I didn't write down her last name." Although I can tell you know her by that smile that's appeared on your face.

"Yeah, Lucy is my sister. I think tomorrow is going to be a busy day. I think I'll try going to sleep now. Thanks Molly. Goodnight."

"Goodnight Mr Christmas."

Chapter 13 Celeste age 9

Today is my ninth birthday. When I woke up this morning the girl that I share a room with, her name is Karen, gave me a birthday card. It was really a bit of paper folded in half but it said happy birthday on the front of it. Karen is older than me, she is ten so she isn't in my class, but she does go to my school.

I've been here for ten weeks now, I don't know why but I thought it was important to know so I keep count of the days. On my first night here I was feeling lonely and a bit scared so I started talking to Karen, I told her about the other girls at school being mean to me and she said she would wipe the smiles off their silly faces, I asked her if she wanted to use my new flannel but she laughed at me. I got cross then and told her everyone always laughed at me and it wasn't nice. I felt like I wanted to cry but I didn't want Karen to think I was a baby so I bit my tongue really hard to stop myself from crying.

The next day at school during lunchtime the usual girls were being horrible to me in the playground, they flicked my hair with a stick and made faces at me and Tom, just like they always do. I looked across the playground and I saw Karen was watching me, I smiled but I don't think she saw me because she looked away. Tom asked who I was smiling at and when I went to point to Karen to show him she had gone. Tom is the only friend I have, last week he was ill and couldn't come to school, it was horrible, I was all by myself for three days, the next time Tom is off school ill I want to catch it too so I don't have to be at school all by myself.

That night Karen told me she would take me under her wing, she said nobody would ever be mean to me again. She said she would teach me how to look after myself and she would tell me everything that I needed to know about growing up and surviving in this world. I went to sleep feeling much happier but I was a bit worried about why Karen had wings.

Chapter 14 Lucy

I really didn't think I'd be able to sleep, my body is an equal measure of excitement and fear, with a dose of apprehension mixed in too, yet somehow I've managed a straight seven hours sleep. Chris is still sleeping soundly next to me and as it's now only just six o'clock I leave him sleeping while I do something I haven't done in ages. I slip out of bed and I pull on my running kit, pleased that it still fits me. Then as quietly as I can I fetch Lupo whose wagging tail tells me that he remembers what my trainers mean. I close the front door quietly behind us and then I gently break into a run, Lupo is happily jogging along side me.

It's the best way that I've ever found to clear my head, while I'm running I concentrate on my breathing, trying to breathe slowly and deeply. The music is playing in my ears, powering me along. While I am out here in the fresh air there's no room for anything else, all I can think about is my feet pounding their familiar rhythm on the pavement as I pass street after street. I'm not thinking about where I'm going, I don't need to because my brain remembers our route, I pass by the familiar houses and shops, then I take a turn up the hill past the church, my legs are struggling now, working harder than they have done in months.

After the second mile we pause briefly at the park so Lupo can run for a bit off his lead, I throw a stick for him to run and fetch while I catch my breath, my lungs are burning and it takes a few minutes for my breathing to regulate, then I stretch out my muscles, preparing them for the next few miles. We are soon on our way again retracing our earlier steps, I wonder why I stopped running, it was lack of time I think. I had forgotten how much I enjoyed the solitude and the feeling of freedom running gives me.

Back at home, I creep into the house, it's still only seven o'clock and I don't expect anyone else to be awake yet. I feed Lupo then get a pot of coffee on to filter while I go for a shower. I stand for too long under the hot water letting the steam melt away some of the tension that has built up in my muscles. Back in our room Chris is just waking up, he looks like he would happily go back to sleep but when he sees me up and ready he starts to get up too.

"Coffee should be ready by now, are you coming down or shall I bring you one up?" I ask him.

He looks at the time before answering "I'll jump in the shower then I'll be down, I'm guessing you will want to get going soon?"

"Yep, I'm almost ready, although do I look okay? I'm not sure what to wear." I tell him.

"You look fine; we are going to a hospital Lucy, not out for dinner. Now, as you said you are ready how about making me some toast?" He says with a mischievous wink.

"Okay, but only because I love you."

"Love you too." But then his face turns serious "Are you going to be okay if this Callum turns out to be someone different to who you are expecting?"

I sit down heavily beside him and answer with a sigh. It's the same question I've been asking myself and I still don't have an answer.

"He already is someone different, to begin with he was a ghost, a stranger, and then he was an imaginary friend that I had as a child, now though, he is back to being a real person who could also be my brother."

And then because the situation is so crazy we both burst out laughing. I sit beside him quietly for a moment then I leave him to get ready while I go and make his breakfast. I feel bad that I won't be spending the day with the children but I know they will be fine with my parents. While I wait for Chris I keep myself busy by making sandwiches, we can take a few with us because Chris will no doubt be hungry and there's plenty for the others to have for lunch, I've wrapped them up and put them in the fridge.

While Chris eats his toast I get the breakfast things out ready for the others when they wake up, I'm trying to make the day as easy as I can for my parents. My stomach is so knotted I'm not hungry but I nibble on a granola bar because I know I should have something.

"Mummy," I hear from the top of the stairs "Mummy, are you here?"

"I'm here my gorgeous girl, are you okay?" I say walking up to meet her. "How about I read you a story before I have to go?"

"Yes please, can it be the princess one?"

As we are about to start the story Harrison wanders in too so I snuggle up to both of them and read the princess story for the hundredth time. I can hear that my mum and dad are up now so I take the children down for their breakfast. Jasmine and Harrison are delighted to see their grandparents are sitting at the table fully dressed and ready for the day ahead.

"Okay my little people; please be good for Nan and Granddad. I'm not sure how long we'll be gone but we'll be home as soon as we can."

"Mummy, I am always good and I'll make sure Harrison is good too." Jasmine tells me, she is trying her hardest to look grown up.

Mum and dad give me a hug as we leave, they don't

say much because I don't think they know what to say. I hug them back tightly and for a moment I think how easy it would be just to stay here and keep life as it is, but then I remind myself that I really might have a brother.

It looks like it's going to be a nice clear day, the sun is just coming up as we begin our journey. Unknown to me though, few hundred miles away Sophie and Carrie are also starting their journey to the same hospital.

Chapter 15 Celeste age 11

I'm crying, although I tried my hardest not too. Today I am going to a new home; a family is going to foster me. Karen told me she has been fostered a few times but she always comes back to our big house. I don't know what to expect, I've met them and they are nice people but I like living here with Karen now. The people that have been looking after me here are okay, they wash my school uniform so I always look smart at school and they always give me breakfast and cook me hot food in the evenings. Sometimes they take a few of us out for the day, we went to the beach a while ago but we didn't have chips or ice-cream, just sandwiches out of a big basket.

I am happier here than I was when my daddy looked after me, now that I'm older I realise that my daddy didn't look after me very well at all. I've also been told that my daddy is in prison now. Prison is a big house where all of the bad people go to live. I was told he was responsible for my mummy's death, and he did lots of buying and selling of drugs, sometimes he mixed drugs he bought with other things and then sold them again, I didn't really understand any of that and Linda said I didn't need too. She works somewhere else now so a lady called Diane comes to see me. She is driving me to the new house today.

Diane has a nice shiny red car and she lets me sit in the front with her like a real grown up. My little bag is on the back seat, I hadn't got much to bring with me, just a few clothes and my school things. Diane lets me listen to the radio as we drive, this makes me happy because I like music, I love to sing. I want to be s singer on Top Of The Pops when I grow up.

We drive for a long time and then all of the tall grey concrete buildings begin to disappear, they are replaced by rows of big red brick houses that have trees growing along the edges of the road and flowers growing in the gardens. There isn't any rubbish piled up by the houses, there isn't even any rubbish by the sides of the road. I open the window and the air smells fresh.

The car slows down to turn a corner and then we drive through some tall gates, we go up a little road and park at the front of the biggest house that I have ever seen in real life. It has a big white door with pillars standing on either side of it, there are three floors of windows and it's all so smart, then Diane turns the engine off and the music comes to an end, then she smiles and tells me that this is my new home.

It's so beautiful but I'm more scared than I've ever been before.

Chapter 16 Lucy

"Lucy, wake up, we're here." Chris says as he turns the ignition off and stretches his arms out overhead; it's been a long drive.

I actually woke up a few minutes ago but I've deliberately been keeping my eyes shut, if I'm asleep I won't have to do this. Now that I'm here I'm scared, I don't know why I'm here, why do I think I know this man? He could be anyone, a criminal, a serial killer, or anything. But then the calm part of my brain kicks in and tells me that he could also be my brother. My brother who is also supposed to be dead I remind myself again.

As we enter the hospital I'm hit my the nauseating smell of cleaning products hanging in the air, Chris is looking at the big map on the wall, we know we are looking for Lark ward, on the phone Molly had said it was in the purple area so while Chris finds it I stare into space, lost in the tangle of thoughts that play on a loop in my head.

"Okay, I've got it." He tells me, but I can't move.

"Can we have a coffee first? I just need a minute if you don't mind?"

"We can do whatever you need to do." He says while looking at the map again to find the nearest coffee shop. He locates it and takes my hand as we go in search of caffeine to fuel me.

Sophie

As we enter the ward a nurse looks up from the nurses' station. I make my way over and tell her we are here to see Jack Hemmingsway, and that a lady called Wendy phoned me to say that she wanted to see us first. She leads us through to a room labelled family room and goes to find Wendy. Neither Carrie nor I can sit still, we just want to see Jack to see if he is alright. It's only a few minutes later when an older nurse comes in and introduces herself as Wendy. In my impatience to see Jack I'm leaping to my feet and jumping in front of her as soon as she is through the door.

"Hello, it's nice to meet you Wendy, I'm Sophie, Jacks sister, and this is his girlfriend Carrie."

"Hello ladies, well, like I said on the phone, Jack was involved in an accident. Unfortunately he was struck by a car late on Friday night."

She doesn't register our gasps but continues to tell us that he has a broken arm, a broken leg, and several broken ribs, they have all been treated and should heal well with no lasting problems, but, the biggest concern is that he also sustained a nasty bump to the head which is still causing him some problems. Carrie has grasped my hand, she looks close to tears.

"What kind of problems?" We ask her in unison.

She glances at her paperwork then looks straight at us and says "Well, when he came in he was unconscious but he regained consciousness within twenty-four hours which is a good sign. But this is where the problems begin."

We are both leaning forwards in our chairs waiting for whatever is coming next. She tells us "Unfortunately, Jack seems to believe his name is Callum. He is refusing to believe he is in actual fact Jackson Hemmingsway. The doctor is hoping that seeing his family will help restore his memories, we would need further tests to confirm it but he may have trauma induced amnesia, meaning that he doesn't want to remember anything that may upset him further. Is there anything in his past that he may not want to remember, has anything bad happened to him recently?"

We are both shaken by this revelation but we tell her that he was fine, Carrie had spent the day before the accident with him and he was perfectly happy, with no problems or worries of any kind. We tell Wendy that as it's a lot to take in could we just have a moment before we go and see him. I can't believe he doesn't know who he is.

"That's fine. I will be back for you in a moment, I just have another family to talk to and then I'll come back to take you through to him." She smiles at us as she leaves.

"Callum." Says Carrie, "Who is this Callum? They must have got Jack muddled with someone else."

"That's exactly what I was thinking, if it isn't Jack in that bed it that means that we are back to not knowing where he is. Unless for some odd reason Jack really does think he is called Callum, but why would he think that?"

The minutes seem to fly by because before we have processed what she has told us Wendy is back to take us to see Jack.

"Okay ladies; are you ready to see Jackson now?"

"Yes, thank you Wendy." We say as we stand to follow her down the corridor.

"I should warn you he won't answer to Jack, only to Callum." We nod our understanding to her but to us it is just a motion, we are far from understanding the situation.

As soon as we enter the ward I can see him, or the bit of him that isn't wrapped in bandages. Carrie has zoomed in on him too, and I can see the smile breaking out on her face. I'm holding back a bit because the name Callum is starting to mean something to me, I just don't know what, but the more I say it the more meaningful it becomes. Jack appears to be sleeping but as we near his bed he opens his eyes.

"Jack, I was so worried about you." Says Carrie winding herself around him, her coppery curls are tumbling forwards and covering his face, she eventually pulls back and strokes his hair. He is smiling but something is off.

"Hi there, I get the feeling I know you but I don't actually remember who you are." He says grinning as she reluctantly releases him.

Carrie staggers back into the chair and I give her shoulder a gentle squeeze as I have my turn, I move closer to his bed.

"So, what about me then Jack do you have any memories of me?"

He doesn't answer straight away, and as the seconds tick by I feel his eyes digging deep into me and I can almost see him thinking. I'm saying a silent prayer, willing him to remember something, anything, no matter how insignificant it might be.

"I know you, but don't be cross because I'm not sure of your name. I remember playing with you as a child, I also remember you as a younger version of who you are now. You look different to how I was remembering you though." He looks at me again then stuns me by saying "You must be Lucy."

Lucy, what's he talking about, the nurse was right about that bump on his head. Carrie looks as though she too is struggling to know what to say or do.

"Jack, I'm Sophie, your sister. And you've been with Carrie for just over a year now." I get out my phone and scroll back through my pictures as far back as I can. I show Jack pictures of himself with Daisy when she was born, there are pictures of him at my wedding, there's not much response from him as I continue to describe each picture although I can see him looking carefully at every detail. When I get to a picture of our parents he gets incredibly frustrated.

"They are not my parents, my mum has got really long hair, and it was very pale and wavy, she looks nothing like this woman."

Well he's right about one thing; the woman in the picture has never had long pale hair. Mum has always had her dark brown hair cut shoulder length at its longest, and she's often said it wasn't made to hold a curl. We come to the end of my pictures so Carrie shows him some of hers, there are pictures of them on nights out and from trips at the weekends. I decide to give them a bit of time alone together and I go in search of some water.

I find a water machine outside in the corridor and then I sit sipping the cold water and breathing deeply trying to calm myself down, I don't know why but I'm shaking, and I can't stop. I keep hearing that name in my head, Callum. Callum. Callum.

A few minutes later Carrie joins me, she slumps down into the seat next to me and I see that there are tears in her eyes, she's clearly feeling as confused as I am. We decide to let Jack rest for a bit, we need some fresh air and a chance to decide on what to do next before we go back in to see him again.

Lucy

"Right, I'm ready," I tell Chris for the third time in the last ten minutes. "I'm sure this time, so let's go before

I change my mind again." We make our way through the maze of corridors that will ultimately lead us to Callum, my legs are shaking and I'm finding it hard to breathe. Lark ward is easy to find and we are there within seconds. Chris stops to talk to a nurse as we enter, she doesn't seem keen to help us. Then I remember.

"Molly, can we talk to Molly please? We've spoken to her on the phone." With a huff she reluctantly agrees to bleep Molly. While we are waiting I look around the ward. I don't realise my feet are moving until I'm standing in front of his bed. Callum looks up from a phone and breaks into a broad smile.

"Lucy, I can't believe it's you. I've missed you so much."

I can't speak, I'm crying so hard that tears are running unchecked down my face, and Callum's too.

We both fall still, we are inches away from each other, just looking at each other's faces and taking in every last detail. I know this face so well because he looks just like me. Chris can obviously see it too because he is looking back and forth between the two of us in amazement.

"Oh my!" Says a voice from behind me "I'm guessing you must be the sister, Callum didn't say that you were twins."

"Pardon." I manage to croak out "Twins, did you say twins?"

"Yeah, of course we are Lucy, what's wrong with you?"

Instinctively I climb up and lay down next to him on the bed. Twins, she said twins, I think she's right. I hold onto my brother for the first time in years, I can't believe I ever forgot I had a brother. Chris calmly pulls the chair up close to the bed and talks to Callum while I cling to him, absorbing the moment.

Chris tells him that I've had dreams about a little boy called Callum for years, then a few days ago I saw him as he is now, then I was told I had an imaginary friend called Callum, then he shocks me by pulling the copy of the newspaper article out of his pocket. He silently hands it to Callum to read. I find another chair and squeeze up as close to the bed as I can, he is reading and rereading the articles and shaking his head just as I did.

"So I'm dead?" He asks.

"Well, apparently not, but a few things really don't make any sense, I know this is all a bit crazy but I know in my heart that I'm your sister, I have such clear memories of us being together when we were very little."

"Me too," Says Callum, "The other problem is that the doctors have been telling me I am called Jack, well, Jackson Hemmingsway to be exact, but I don't know who he is."

"But you are Callum." I tell him.

"I know, that's what I keep saying too but they don't believe me Lucy, maybe now that you are here they might listen."

"Jack." Whispers a voice from the other side of the bed, I had seen the women approaching but thought they were here for someone else; one of them is sitting on the edge bed now. I'm about to ask who they are when Molly comes back over.

"Okay folks, visiting clearly states only two visitors at a time. So who's leaving?"

"Will you stay sis?" Says Callum.

"Of course I will." I say.

The problem is, one of the other women has just said exactly the same thing. I reach for Callum's hand and as politely as I can I tell the other two women to maybe come back later.

"I'm not going anywhere," The dark haired one says. "He's my brother."

"Umm, no. Callum is my brother, we haven't seen each other in a very long time but he is my brother, I'm feeling quite emotionally overwhelmed and I really don't want to be rude but if you and your other friend could come back later that would be great."

She doesn't look happy, neither does the quiet red head, she looks incredibly upset. The one that says she's his sister looks me squarely in the eyes as she talks to me.

"There is clearly a mix up somewhere but this man is my brother Jack, I am Sophie, and this is Jacks girlfriend Carrie. You've just admitted it's been a while since you last saw your brother so obviously you are mistaken." Then she shows me some photos on her phone taken of them together over the years. I feel deflated, my happy bubble has just been popped, it seems too cruel to think that maybe he isn't my brother after all. I feel broken; I just want to go home now.

"I'm sorry. I really don't understand what's going on." I tell her, and honestly I'm more confused than ever. Chris puts his arm around me and then I see he is rummaging in my bag. He writes both of our phone numbers on the back of one of the news articles and gives them back to Callum.

"Sophie, Carrie. Sorry about this. But as you can clearly see, your Jack, our Callum, does look a lot like my wife, Callum says they are twins. Lucy was adopted at the age of three and she truly believes this man is her brother, he has already confirmed it. We will go now to give you some time together but I've left our numbers in case you want to talk to us anymore. Maybe when the bump on his head goes down things will become clearer, and then hopefully we can all begin to make sense of this situation.

Both Carrie and Sophie stand and watch as I kiss Callum goodbye, he hugs me with his good arm and I whisper to him that I can come back soon if he remembers anything else. I avoid eye contact with the other two women, I can feel the anger coming off the dark haired one, Sophie. Just as we are leaving the ward Chris doubles back and asks her,

"Were you adopted as well?"

"No, of course not, that's absurd." Is Sophie's instant reply. Carrie however looks unsure what to think, because she has been thinking the resemblance between the woman called Lucy and her Jack is quite striking, she can see that they could easily be twins.

Chapter 17 Celeste age 11

I've been living with Mr and Mrs Western for three days now. They are called Emma and Steven. They are really nice although they are older than my real mum and dad. Steven is a surgeon and Emma likes to make their house nice, she also goes out to help with charities, I asked her what that was and she said it just means she likes to help people. I haven't been to school since I've been here because it is the half term, Halloween is coming soon and Emma says she will buy some sweets and costumes for us all.

Steven goes out to work very early every morning, he smells really nice and dresses in very smart clothes, he gave me a kiss on the top of my head this morning as he was leaving and told me to have fun, he always gives Emma a kiss before he goes out too, and again when he comes home at night.

I asked Emma what Steven was talking about when he told me to have fun, she told me that we were going to do some shopping. We got in her car and drove for a while with the radio on, she likes to sing along to the music too. She took me to lots of different shops and I was allowed to choose any clothes that I liked. We carried armfuls of clothes into a little room in a shop called H&M, she said I had to try them on to make sure they would fit. It was so much fun. She let me have so many clothes. Then she asked if I wanted to have a little haircut, I wasn't sure about that because once when my daddy cut my hair the children at school laughed at me a lot, but I told her I would have a haircut because I knew that's what she wanted me to say.

We went to a special shop that does hair cutting. I sat in a special chair that went up in the air, and then they put a strange coat on me so that the hair didn't itch me. Emma spoke to the lady before she started then another lady gave Emma a cup of tea. I was waiting for her to get the scissors out but she brushed my hair then I had to walk across the shop where I sat at a funny little sink where the lady washed my hair, I could smell apples which reminded me of my mummy. When my hair was clean she washed it again so I thought maybe it was very dirty but she said this was something called conditioner that would take the tangles away.

When we left the hair cutting shop I kept swishing my head backwards and forwards, my hair was so soft, I looked at my reflection every time we passed a shop window, the lady had made my hair look so nice, it doesn't touch my bottom anymore, it's just past my shoulders but I love my haircut and my new clothes. I think I might love Emma too.

It is Christmas day today; I am feeling a bit sleepy because last night I was allowed to stay up late because Emma and Steven had some of their friends round for a Christmas party. There was so much food, and lots of bottles of wine that fizzed in the glass when it was poured, I was allowed to try a little bit and the bubbles went up my nose and made me giggle. Emma bought me a new dress, red for Christmas she said. It was a brilliant party with lots of music and singing too. I went to bed much later than I normally do and although the party was still happening downstairs I fell straight to sleep.

This morning when I woke up there was a red stocking hanging at the end of my bed. I peered into it not sure what I would find. It was amazing, there were little presents all wrapped up in shiny gold paper, I wasn't sure if I should open them but I was so excited that I opened the tiny one, it was a lip gloss, just like the one that Emma wears, I was just wondering about opening another little present when there was a light tapping at my door and Emma and Steven came in. She was so excited that I had opened the lip gloss she told me to open them all. I got some Santa socks, some shower gel and shampoo, I have my own bathroom in this house with lots of space for all of my new things, there was also a pack of pens and a new pencil case. I've never had any Christmas presents before.

Emma tells me to come downstairs with them and see what's under the tree. I follow them down where the tree lights are twinkling and there is a pile of presents sitting underneath their beautiful tree. They have given me a new school bag, some more clothes and pyjamas and a beautiful gold necklace of a butterfly. I feel so happy, I fling myself into Emma's arms and tell them both thank you. Then I feel sad because I'm scared they will send me back because I haven't got anything to give them.

Chapter 18 Sophie

The question about the adoption has been slowly pushing itself to the front of my mind as I am driving home from the hospital. We made a stop at Carries flat to collect a few bits that she needed for the next few days because we have decided that she is coming back home with me. We both feel it's best to deal with the Jack situation together as a team. She's fallen asleep now so while I'm driving I'm replaying the conversation from the hospital, clearly Jack believes he is called Callum, I'm equally convinced that poor Lucy honestly believes that Jack is her brother Callum, there's no denying the similarity between them, in any other situation I would have thought they were obviously related.

Something about the adoption question somehow rings a few bells though, as does the name Callum, although it's a common enough name, maybe I'm thinking of another Callum. I try to distract myself from my niggling thoughts of Jack by listening to the radio but to no great success. I feel both mentally and physically drained as we arrive back home, I can see Carrie does too, she actually looks terrible. Josh must have seen us pull up because he's waiting for us at the front door, I had phoned him earlier from the hospital to let him know we were on our way home but told him the situation was far too complicated to talk about over the phone. I said I'd update him when I was home, I know he is worried too.

Josh has known Jack for years, they met at university playing for the same cricket team, and it was at one of their rare victory parties in the pub one night that I had met Josh. My brother has always liked reminding me how I have him to thank for what he calls my happy ending. He might be a bit of a joker sometimes who is always late, forgets birthdays, and never takes anything too seriously but he's also one of the nicest, loving, decent people you could ever meet. I ask myself again why this had to happen to him but although his brain is obviously still traumatised from the accident I'm grateful that he is otherwise going to be okay. When I think what could have happened to him I shudder.

Carrie offers to make us all dinner tonight so that I can spend some time with Daisy, an offer that I gratefully accept. Daisy wants us to make a bracelet with a kit she was given for Christmas so that's what we do for the next hour, being with her blocks out everything else. She is telling me all about her day with her daddy, then she sings me some songs that she had learnt at school before the holidays, it's a fun hour together but I still need to tell Josh what's going on, there hasn't been chance yet.

It turns out that Carrie is a great cook, she's produced an amazing turkey and pasta dish using ingredients that I didn't know I had lurking in my kitchen cupboards. Daisy hugs her when she has finished eating and says it was the best meal she has ever had, Carrie seems to be her favourite person at the moment, a point which is proven a bit later on when Daisy asks if auntie Carrie can put her to bed and read her a bedtime story, Carries happily obliges and they go upstairs together hand in hand.

Once we are alone Josh takes a chilled bottle of wine from the fridge and pours us each a glass, then he tells me he wants to know everything about the hospital visit. I wander through to the lounge and make myself comfortable then I tell him everything about the visit from start to finish. Once I'm done he takes a deep breath and says,

"Well I wasn't expecting that, what do we do now?"

"I really don't know." I tell him as I wedge myself in and curl up under his arm. We sit quietly for a few minutes each lost in our own thoughts before I break the silence.

"I've been thinking a lot about what Lucy asked about the adoption. Jack doesn't look anything like me, or mum or dad, maybe Lucy and Chris are right to have asked that question. Maybe it's a question we should be asking, what if it's true that Jack was adopted and poor Lucy lost her brother for all those years."

"I have to admit that when Jack first introduced you as his sister I was surprised, he's almost the opposite of you, is Lucy very much like him?"

"Yes, she is, she is exactly as I imagine Jack would have looked if he was a girl, their colouring is identical, the curve of their noses, everything is the same. If they aren't related I would be amazed."

Then I start thinking how Josh is right, Jack and I are nothing alike in anyway, it's then that I realise that I might have lost my brother and as the emotions of the day bombard me my tears start to flow.

"Sorry, I didn't mean to interrupt." Says Carrie, she is looking awkward upon seeing me crying. She's standing in the doorway and looks as though she doesn't know whether to stay or go.

"Daisy is fast asleep. I'll get out of your way." And she turns to go.

"You're not interrupting anything, come and join us, its nice having you here. I've just been updating Josh on everything. I just hope Jack's memory comes back sooner rather than later so we can all get on with our lives."

Its then that I notice her gently touching her stomach, something she's done a lot over the last few days, she catches me looking and nods. Josh looks totally bemused so she confirms it.

"I'm pregnant, Jack doesn't know yet, I was going to tell him on Christmas day. I got him a present, it's a key chain that says Daddy. Now she's crying uncontrollably too. I can't imagine how hard this is for her, I'm an emotional wreck at the moment with all the worry and she's got pregnancy hormones flooding her body to deal with as well. I give her a big hug and tell her it will be okay, even if it takes a while to get Jack back on track she will have us to support her. Josh is a man of few words so he gives her a kiss on the forehead and offers to make her a cup of tea.

"I'm so grateful for all you are doing Sophie, thank you so much, I really don't think I could have got through the last few days without you." She says.

"Well, Josh and I are here for you and the baby whenever you need us, we will get through this, it might take a while longer than I had hoped to get Jack back on track but it will all be alright in the end, his memory will come back and I'm sure he will be thrilled to be a dad."

"Don't forget, you are going to be an auntie too." She says smiling. And she sips her tea looking more relaxed than she has all day.

In my head I'm busy planning our next move. If Jack hasn't regained his memory in a few days time I will need to have a serious talk with my parents. Josh is right, Jack and I are polar opposites of each other, and he is absolutely nothing like either of our parents either, in looks or mannerisms. I really am starting to think he was adopted. Or maybe I was, something isn't right.

Carrie goes off to bed while Josh and I watch a film, I'm trying to watch it but it's hard to concentrate on the plot because my mind is elsewhere. I can remember Jack being there for all of my life so if he is adopted he must have been a baby when he came. It's funny the fragments I can remember now that I'm thinking about it, I'm almost taking myself back in time. Jack was always called Jackson when he was little, then he was really ill and I wasn't allowed to play with him for a while, I can't remember what was wrong with him though. Then as we grew up we were always together, he was my best friend as well as my brother.

I fill up my wine glass and dig deep into the Christmas chocolates hoping to find one of the good ones left. I have to stop my brain from mentally going around in circles, I briefly wonder how Lucy is tonight. Then I decide to call the hospital to see if there is any change in Jack's condition, I go upstairs to make the call so that I won't disturb Josh. They tell me he is sleeping but there is no significant change since we left him, Wendy says he has slept for hours.

Lucy

"So what do you want to do next Lucy?" Chris asks me as we are nearing home, I've been lost in my thoughts since we left the hospital and I hadn't realised how long we had been travelling.

"Do you mean right now next? Or over the next few days? Because right now I really don't think I have the energy to do much more than stop for takeaway, break open a bottle of wine and lose myself in a movie with the kids."

"Okay, that's a good enough plan for now, but you know we'll have to talk about Callum, or Jack, at some point?"

"Yes, I know, but just not tonight okay?"

"Okay, that's a deal. Now what shall we get, Chinese or Indian?"

I know that he prefers Chinese while I always chose Indian. So I say "Whatever we get to first." Knowing that his favourite Chinese takeaway is just around the corner.

Walking through the door at home I can hear noises coming from upstairs so I go and see what's happening. I follow the loudest noise to the bathroom where Jasmine is in the bath singing to my mum at the top of her voice, meanwhile my dad is next door with Harrison getting him into his new dinosaur pyjamas.

"Hello there, what's going on up here?" I ask.

As predicted its Jasmine that answers me "Well Mummy, we made cakes as a surprise for you and we got so messy that Nana said we had to get cleaned up, I didn't make much mess at all, it was really all Harrison's mess really Mummy."

"Oh, was it really Jasmine?" I say breaking into a giggle. "Daddy stopped and got a Chinese feast so why don't you go and get dressed and I'll get food ready."

"Yay, I love China food." She declares and she's leaping out of the bath to get dressed and soaking my mum in the process. Mum wipes the bubbles off her arms with a towel and asks me if I am alright, I almost say I'm fine, it's my automatic response but I realise that I am not fine. I tell her I just want to get changed into something more comfortable and if she is okay with Jasmine, I will see her downstairs in a few minutes for dinner.

Chris has laid out plates and the food is keeping warm in the oven, he's sitting at the dining table with a beer in his hand and I notice how tired he looks.

"Thank you for today." I tell him while I massage his shoulders for a few moments before sitting down next to him.

"I'm just worried about what the next step is and how it will affect you." He tells me before passing me a drink.

"I've no idea what's next but let's forget about it for now and eat." I say. The smells coming from the oven are amazing and I remember I didn't eat anything for lunch, Chris ate the sandwiches we took with us and a muffin from the coffee shop but I couldn't eat anything. I realise I've almost finished my beer and I get myself a large glass of water before laying out the Chinese feast.

"This is very nice, thank you." Says my mum, looking longingly at the feast I am putting out on the table, I know she is desperate to ask more but will be waiting for the children to go to bed.

The six of us easily demolish the banquet meant for eight people, and then we are very lazy and watch a movie with the children. When the film finishes I can't help but wish life always came with a happy ending no matter what obstacles were thrown in along the way.

Chris and I take the children up to bed and supervise as they wash sauce off their faces and brush their teeth. I read Harrison his story while Chris reads to Jasmine. Once cuddly toys have been arranged and lights turned off we make our way back down, if it wasn't for mum and dad being here I would be under my duvet by now, I think Chris would happily go to bed now too.

"So what happened today? Did you meet Callum?" My mum asks me the moment we enter the room, I take a deep breath and sink into the sofa.

"You look like you need this." My dad says handing each of us a whisky.

"Thanks Dad, well, there's another twist to the story of Callum because it turns out his sister Sophie says that he is called Jack." I say stunning my parents into silence. I'm suddenly incredibly cold so I sit in front of the fire on a pile of cushions, I am gently stroking Lupo's soft fur while I talk them through the day. I start at the very beginning but it is really quite difficult when I'm unsure of so much myself.

"Lucy love, I really don't mean to upset you or add to any of this but are you sure you haven't just muddled a few memories, I mean, well, a dream or a vision or whatever it was doesn't really compare to someone else having a lifetime of memories and pictures of someone does it? Do you think you could have got this all wrong?"

That's the question I've been asking myself ever since I left the hospital, all logic points to Sophie being his true sister and I'm so tired I've started making up an imaginary world in my head. I can't face answering my mum's question right now, it's too hard, so instead I top up my whisky, kiss them all goodnight and leave the room, dragging my heavy heart behind me.

Chapter 19 Celeste age 13

Emma and Steven said they needed to talk to me, we are going to have a family meeting, I have to come straight home and not go to the park with my friends after school like I normally do. I go to a new school now where I have lots of new friends. Yesterday was my 13th birthday and I was allowed to have all of my friends here and Emma made us pizza and ice-cream, then we had the biggest chocolate birthday cake that I had ever seen, it had sparkly candles and crumbled chocolate flakes sprinkled on top of it.

When I get home they are both sitting at the breakfast bar in the kitchen, there is another lady there too, I think she is the lady called Debbie who came to see me a few times when I first came here. Emma makes me a drink and a snack like she always does when I come home and then I sit with them as the lady tells me that Emma and Steven would like to adopt me, this means that I will never have to live anywhere else ever again.

Then the lady asks to see my room so I take her upstairs, then she asks me if I would like Emma and Steven to be my new parents, I tell her that I would,

I'm so happy living here. I wonder if they would let Karen come and live here too.

Chapter 20 Susan 1988

"Jackson, Sophie, I've made a picnic for lunch with all of your favourite sandwiches in. Can you pick the last few strawberries then we can go and surprise Daddy, he is working out in the empty old field today."

"Can I bring my truck Mummy?" Asks Jackson

"Yes of course you can little man, are you ready Sophie?"

"Here I am Mummy, Jamima is coming too."

"I thought she would, but she really needs a wash soon, maybe we can put her in the sink later for a good wash and then I'll hang her on the line to dry in the sunshine." Jamima is an old rag doll, she has become increasingly floppy recently and probably needs a bit of new stuffing, and despite having newer dolls Jamima is still Sophie's favourite.

"Okay Mummy, she can have a bath, but she has to be dry for bedtime or I will never be able to go to sleep without her." Says Sophie very seriously.

I really don't want to risk her not being dry in time for Sophie's bed time because that would be a disaster. "Mmm, well then, let's wash her tomorrow morning as soon as you wake up then so she will have all day to dry."

"Okay Mummy." Smiles Sophie.

"Daddy is in the empty old field by the woods fixing some fencing. I've got food, drinks and a blanket, you both need to get your sun hats on then we can go because I think Daddy will be getting very hungry."

It is a beautiful sunny day at the beginning of September. The campsite has just a few visitors left, and there are a couple of campers picking apples in the orchards in exchange for a free night or two. School starts tomorrow, Sophie will be going up to the next stage and Jackson is due to start, so today is their last day of the holidays so I want it to be an extra special day.

Peter sees us as soon as we enter the field, probably alerted to us by the noise the children are making, they are singing at the top of their little voices. Peter is happy to see us with the basket of food. We choose a shaded spot under the old oak tree that sits proudly in the middle of the field.

At the bottom end of the field is an area of rough overgrown woodland that we are deciding what to do with, we are thinking maybe a picnic area for the campers, or maybe we will just fence it off so it looks tidy and leave it to nature, the camping has become so popular we had thought of turning this field into another smaller camping site, it could share the amenities with the site next door. The extra income would be welcome and it shouldn't make too much more work for us.

We eat sandwiches, cakes, sausage rolls, and strawberries, all things the children had asked for. Peter and I also indulge in a glass or two of the new cider we are experimenting in making. It's idyllic just sitting here in the sun, Peter and I lay down on our backs looking up at the leaves blowing in the breeze, just like we used to do years ago, back when we were making our plans for the future, Jackson and Sophie are happily playing and chatting beside us.

Sophie is telling Jackson all about school again, and she makes him practice answering her pretend register. She tells him that he will soon learn all about letters and numbers so he can be as clever as she is.

"Sophie, Mummy and Daddy are asleep."

"Shh Jackson, don't wake them, shall we play hide and seek?"

"I find you." Jackson says before covering his eyes with his chubby little hands and counting clumsily to twenty. He repeats numbers one to three a few times then as he shouts out twenty and opens his eyes he has a careful look around, he takes a few steps back towards the entrance to the field and then changes his mind and goes in the opposite direction towards the woods, after a few more steps he can see movement, he carefully creeps a bit closer to where he can see Sophie's pink hair bow poking up above a bush on the edge of the woods so he runs over to her shouting "Got you."

Sophie is not happy at being found so soon, she thought that had been a good hiding place. Reluctantly she takes her turn to be the seeker, she closes her eyes and begins her count to twenty. She get as far as eighteen when she hears a scream that makes her blood run cold.

"Susan, wake up!"

"What is it Peter?" Then after looking around the panic rises and she cries "Where are the children?"

They are both on their feet now, instinctively running towards the woods; Peter is running towards where he thinks the scream came from. Sophie is standing in the middle of a clearing calling for Jackson at the top of her voice.

"Mummy, Daddy, Jackson went to hide, I heard him screaming but I can't find him."

Susan's eyes are frantically searching for her son as

she scrambles under branches and through the tangled maze of trees, her mother's instinct is on high alert, she has to find her baby.

Peter is more practical, he calmly asks Sophie where Jackson was before he went off to hide, she shows us the spot he was standing so we work in a circle spiralling out from that point, because he can't have gone far in the time it takes to count to twenty. After a few minutes with no sign of him panic is really setting in.

Suddenly Peter comes to an abrupt halt and his hands go to his head as he sinks to his knees amongst the brambles, he is letting out a high pitched wail, he sounds like a wounded animal.

Chapter 21 Celeste almost 14

Emma has been acting strangely for a few weeks now, she cries a lot and Steven leaves the room whenever I come in. I think I have done something wrong but I don't know what. I keep my room tidy, I work hard at school and I always come home by the time they tell me to.

Today is Saturday so I don't have to get up yet. I'm lying in bed watching TV when Steven knocks on my door, he never comes in without knocking, that's something they taught me. He asks me if I could come down for a chat, I put my hoodie on over my pyjamas and go to find them. Emma looks like she has been crying, her eyes are all red and her skin is blotchy, she has a tissue bunched up in her hand that she is fiddling with, she hasn't noticed but pieces are falling like confetti to the floor.

They tell me that unfortunately they are unable to proceed with the adoption. I ask what that means, Steven seems a bit muddled with his words but then he tells me I will have to go back to the children's home. I feel like my world is falling down around me, this can't be happening, I want to stay here, they said I could stay. I shout that they said I could stay but

Emma just cries some more. I don't know why she is crying, I'm the one that is being sent away. I ask what I've done wrong, Steven looks a bit upset now as he tells me that I haven't done anything wrong, it is just bad timing.

It seems that bad timing means that they tried to get pregnant for years and were unsuccessful. Now though, through some kind of miracle Emma is unexpectedly pregnant, with triplets. They say it would just be too much with three new babies and me. Meaning I am no longer wanted.

They tell me I can stay until the end of the school term because a good education is so important, but end of term is still a few weeks away. I tell them I don't want to stay, if they don't want to keep me. I will go now to make it easier for them, I can't stay here for a few more weeks knowing the end is coming. Emma tells me she is sorry and I let her hug me while she cries because I really want someone to hug me.

Chapter 22 Lucy

We spend a few quiet days at home. The children are both happy playing with their new toys and spending the last few days with their grandparents. Since we have had the children we don't do much for New Years Eve. Mum cooked us a lovely meal of roast pork with all the trimmings followed by the richest chocolate mousse I have ever eaten accompanied by a bottle of champagne. Then later on after we had put the children to bed we watched chat shows and fire works on TV as the New Year landed and the bells rang out.

On New Year's Day we ate all of the leftover cheese from the fridge, finished off any remaining chocolates and stocked up on fresh fruit ready for a healthy start to the New Year. We are almost two days into January now and the children go back to school at the beginning of next week. In some ways the time has flown by but then when I think about all that has happened it feels more like two months than two weeks.

I've been out running each morning with Lupo which is doing me good in more ways than one. I'm sleeping much better now and although after my runs I am exhausted and my limbs hurt I am feeling more energised for the rest of the day. This morning I decide to face another fear and I take an eager Lupo to the river.

I keep a careful distance from the river because I still don't trust its power. I follow the muddy footpath carefully alongside the trees that run along the edge of the river bed, my feet have become accustomed to the new rhythm they have to make on the uneven surface. It's about a mile along the winding path and then it comes to an end where the path opens up into a beautiful meadow, I can see why it is such a popular spot. Lupo enjoys a few minutes freedom bounding through the tall grass before he falls back into step beside me as we go back the same way along the path, it's still early and it is slightly eerie because there is still nobody else around.

There is a strange mist that hovers over the water, silence surrounds me and I feel like I am alone in the world. Halfway back along the path there is an area where the river becomes incredibly shallow, the river bed is very high here so I let Lupo off his leads to paddle in, but despite the freezing temperature he seems to enjoy a brief few seconds paddling then he stands staring down at his reflection.

That's when I swallow my fear and I take a few steps forward and stand rigidly next to him. I gaze down at my reflection too and I am horrified by what I see. Even using the thick murky water as a mirror I can see the dark rings under my eyes and I look as though I've aged five years over the last few weeks. I can almost feel the river pulling me closer, it is taunting me into taking another step towards its clutches. I shiver as I quickly step back onto the path. It would be so easy to slip deep down into the waters hands, to surrender to its power. I ask myself if that's what Callum did, the thought of that sends shivers throughout my body, I turn away from the water and begin to run, I'm keen to leave here now so I pick up the pace, imagining I can hear Callum's screams once again following me as I run as fast as I can towards home.

Over breakfast we chat about what my parents have got planned for the next few weeks, as there is still more snow predicted they can't do much because so many of their hobbies are outside. Mum tells us she has bought a large second hand green house that she plans to fix up so she can grow more vegetables and my dad wants to get back out on his boat, he is even talking of joining a sailing club.

I feel like I am miles away, I can still feel the pull of the river and it is making me feel uneasy, the calm of the surface is mirror smooth, disguising its deadly power, fooling people with its beauty. What did Callum feel as it swept him away, I wonder how long he fought against the force of the unyielding water for before he surrendered? Then my thoughts are disturbed by mum talking to me.

"Lucy, Chris, your dad and I have been talking and we wanted to ask you all if you'd like to come back to ours for a couple of days over this last weekend, to give you a break before school starts and everything gets busy again, you don't have to answer right now, talk it over between you and let us know."

"Thanks Mum, Dad, that's a kind offer." I say, I wasn't expecting that and I'm ashamed to admit I had been looking forward to a few pyjama days before I have to go back to work, luckily I did all of the lesson plans at the beginning of the holiday.

"Well, I think it's a brilliant idea." Chris says looking meaningfully at me, however, I do have a few things I need to take care of for work but we could leave on Friday afternoon, then spend the last weekend with you before work and school starts up again on Tuesday."

"We want to go to Nanny and Granddads house too don't we Harrison?" Jasmine asks her brother who simply nods enthusiastically at her question.

"Okay then Mum, I know you were planning to leave later on today so we'll see you in couple of day's time." I tell her.

"Oh good, that's brilliant news." Says my dad just as my phone starts to ring. While they are all chatting and making plans I take the call upstairs.

"That was Callum," I tell Chris as he sits down beside me on the bed a few minutes later. "He said he still can't get his memory straight although he can remember quite a lot of things now, but the hospital is releasing him because his other injuries are healing fine and he has mastered using his crutches, even with a broken arm."

"That's good, for him I mean, good that he is recovering, it must be frustrating for him though."

"Well, he said that Sophie has been talking to their parents, it seems the question of adoption was one she needed answers too, Callum or Jack or whatever we call him said his parents have something to tell him and he wants me to be there too. Sophie has agreed and we are all due to meet at his parents' house tomorrow, I noted down the address, its miles away but I think we have to go, maybe get some closure on this whole mystery, what do you think?"

"Sorry love," Coughs my mum from the doorway "I didn't mean to listen, I only heard the end bit."

So she comes in and joins us perched on the edge of the bed and says "Well that's easy then, your dad and I can take Jasmine and Harrison back with us this afternoon, we can even take the dog and then you two can join us in a few days time as planned when you've straightened out this....whatever it is. Go and get this poor man some answers."

"Thanks Mum, that would be a great help, I know the children will be happy with you and dad. I really don't know what to expect from all this, I've played out so many scenarios in my head over the last few days but none of them seem at all feasible."

"You go and work this thing out, your dad and I will be fine with the children." And she wraps me in a hug but not before I've caught the worried look that passes fleetingly across her face.

Callum/Jack

I can't seem to get through more than a few hours without falling asleep at the moment, my body appears to be healing well, the doctor said it looked as though I kept myself fit and healthy before the accident which has helped my body through this ordeal. Although my mind is still a bit fuzzy I can remember a little bit more each day, sometimes things come to me when I'm reading the paper or just falling asleep, the less I try to force it my mind seems to work better.

I know that Carrie is upset that I don't remember everything about our relationship but I do know that I feel much better when she is with me, she was happy when I told her that which was a relief, I was worried I'd sounded a bit mushy. I have some memories of being with her but they are still blurred around the edges.

I remember lots about Sophie now, although I can't always get things in the right order, the doctor said that it was to be expected. My parents came to see me in the hospital just before Sophie came to take me home, well, not home exactly, she wants me with her so she can look after me, Carrie is going to spend some time there too because it seems they get on very well together, which is good.

My parents are a bit odd, I recognise them but they almost feel like grandparents, I know who my mother is, I can see her with me and Lucy years ago, these images are so clear they could have been yesterday, I know she liked to sing and her long hair would float in the air as she danced, or maybe I've got her muddled with someone else. I was surprised when they told me I was an accountant, I hadn't given work much thought but I wasn't expecting that to have been my career choice, it sounds a bit dull.

Chapter 23 Celeste age 15

I still miss Emma and Steven sometimes, but then I get cross with myself, I must not allow myself to miss them, they didn't care enough about me to want to keep me so I mustn't waste my time thinking about them. When I came back to the children's home I was pleased to find that Karen was still here, she didn't talk to me for the first few days, she said I thought I was better than her, I said no I didn't, and because I was still upset about being cast aside I was more aggressive than I normally am. I ignored her because I was so angry, but then few days later she walked home from school with me, we are friends again now.

Karen says people always let you down, making promises they can't, or won't keep, I think she is right. I go to the old school again now, Emma and Steven stopped paying for the other one when I left their house. Karen is about to leave school, she is doing her exams, she says it's important to work hard at school, we need to get good jobs so that we never have to be dependent on anyone else ever again.

The weeks and months pass by with nothing much really happening. I really miss my old bedroom, and my own bathroom that I had at Emma and Stevens house, I miss lying in bed and watching TV, and I miss going out for all the nice meals, and trips to the cinema, I miss my old friends too and because I know they won't fit into this life I haven't made any effort to keep in touch with any of them. But most of all I miss feeling like everything was going to be alright.

I work as hard as I can at school and I always make sure my homework is done, I go to the library and I read about topics we are learning about so that I know everything that I possibly can. My teachers are pleased with my work and tell me I should do well in my exams next year, one of my teachers has even been helping me to look at courses at college and helping me to decide what I might like to do. I think I would like to study art and design.

I had a routine and it was okay but now it is all messed up again because I have a new foster family, I don't want to go anywhere else because what's the point? But it seems like my life is out of my control.

I'm driven out to the suburbs again, I wonder if all foster families live outside the city. This family are older parents, they have a daughter who is away at university, she wants to be a vet, and they have a son who is just about to take his exams and finish high school so he's about a year ahead of me. I've met them twice before and they seem like nice people, but I guess everyone seems nice when they are out to impress. They both work, he is a solicitor and she writes cook books, Karen laughed and said I shouldn't be hungry there. I'm going to miss Karen again.

The family are fine, the dad is called Martin, he works quite long hours and when he is at home he is often in his office, the mum is Brenda and she is always in the kitchen either cooking or planning recipes, she's nice. Camilla is the daughter and she comes home sometimes at the weekend, she didn't take much notice of me when we first met which suits me fine. The son is part of every sports team that the school has got, he goes to a different school to me, a better one. He is called Matthew, although only his parents call him that, he likes to be called Matt. He is actually really nice, he said I could go out with him and his friends to a party next weekend. Living here might not be so bad.

My 16th birthday

Martin and Brenda are going to spend the evening with some of their friends, they took me out for a birthday lunch today, and Matt came too. They gave me a voucher for a clothes shop which is nice of them so I think I'll buy a new top. Tonight I am allowed to have a few friends round for a birthday party. They said Matthew has to be here too to look after me, and he has got a few of his friends coming round as well.

Some of Matthews friends sneak in some alcohol, they offer me some but I refuse, I've seen what can happen to your body when you put rubbish in it, although I don't tell them that, I never talk about my real parents, nobody needs to know where I came from, I've noticed people treat me differently if they know my parents took drugs and drank too much alcohol. The party is fun, we play the music as loud as we can and we have pushed the sofa out of the way to make a dance floor.

I've been drinking Pepsi all night but this one tastes funny. My head is spinning and I feel a bit sick. I notice one of Matt's friends is laughing at me, I'm finding it hard to stand still, and I keep swaying. I really don't feel very well so I slip out of the party and go upstairs to my room for a lie down, hopefully I'll be alright in a moment.

I must have fallen asleep because I when I open my eyes I see that Matt is lying on the bed next to me. He said he was worried about me, he thinks one of his mates put some vodka in my drink. He strokes my face ever so gently with his hand, and then he kisses me. He's done this before but this time is different, he gets up and locks the door and then he comes back over to me, my head still feels a bit fuzzy, it's hard to focus, but then I realise that Matt is taking his clothes off.

Chapter 24 Lucy

The day dawns fresh and crisp as we begin our journey to Lavender farm, cobwebs twinkle from the bushes that line the narrow roads while the fields create a stark gleaming white landscape, we spot a deer in one of the fields and it looks like a scene from a Christmas card. As we drive the miles slip away and we fall deeper into the country side. Neither of us knows what to expect from today, I just want an end to this unknowing. During the journey this morning I've read through the news articles time and time again so much so that I've committed them to memory. Chris has been brilliant, sensing when I just need to lose myself in my thoughts.

The sat nav breaks into the silence and announces our arrival telling us our destination is on our left, but the only thing we can see to our left is a narrow lane, although lane might be exaggerating its size considerably. We turn in and follow the bumps and bends until we pull up outside an old red brick house, a house with deep green window frames that I have seen many times before. A sight I wasn't expecting to greet us but it almost makes perfect sense, it takes a moment to steady myself, for so long this image has haunted me. In real life it's bigger and more dominating than it was in my memories. Being here almost feels like I am living in my dream, hopefully it won't turn into the nightmare that normally follows. I can already feel my heart pounding and the panic taking root.

"I've been here before." I tell Chris in barely more than a whisper. "I know this house, there is a dark brown cobbled floor in the hallway that has table full of framed photographs on it, then there is an L shaped staircase running up off to the left and a room with a big fire place opens off to the right of the entrance hall."

"Do you think you've actually physically been here before and you were replaying an old memory or is this another part of the dream?"

"Oh, I've been here before, I'm absolutely sure of it." Then I take a last steadying deep breath and climb out of the car, Chris reaches for my hand and gives me a reassuring squeeze as we make our way towards the big wooden front door, the gravel crunches underfoot as we approach. Almost hidden by shrubs on the wall to the left is an old weather beaten plaque telling us we are at Lavender farm. The whole place has an unearthly ghostly feel to it.

I ring the old rusty doorbell and hear the heavy chimes echoing from deep inside the house. Sophie is the one who greets us and leads us inside, she looks like she hasn't been sleeping well, but she greets us with a smile and thanks us for making the journey. She takes our coats and puts them in a cupboard that stands at the foot of the staircase before leading us down the hallway, past the room with the big fire place. We go through to the back of the house, to a part I also remember clearly, I sniff the air, almost expecting to smell cookies.

We enter a large room kitchen at the back of the house and find the others sitting around an old wooden dining table. Carrie looks uncomfortable but nothing compares to the horror on the faces of the older couple who are looking nervously down at the table. Introductions are needless because it's obvious that they are Sophie's parents, there is no mistaking it, she has clearly inherited her mother's height and colouring, the mother, although sitting hunched over in her chair has a long back giving away her height, she still has dark hair even though its streaked through with sprigs of grey, the dad is balding but his facial hair is still dark, they paint a stark contrast to Callum who looks blonder than ever in comparison.

"Mum, Dad, this is Lucy and her husband Chris. Lucy, Chris, these are my parents, Peter and Susan." Sophie says with an obvious touch of nervousness creeping into her voice.

The old couple look at each other first for a long moment before looking up in our direction, when they look at me properly for the first time I know they can see it, they know Callum is my brother. Susan gasps and seems to disappear into herself, Carrie hands her a glass of water which she sips gratefully, her trembling hands almost lose their grip on the glass.

There's coffee and tea set out on the table along with a water jug and it reminds me of a meeting, or a conference, although I suppose that's kind of what this is. Callum stands up and tries to give me a hug, not easy when you are holding onto crutches with a broken arm, but it's a gesture I appreciate. I hold onto him thinking again how he feels like such an important part of me.

"I'm so glad you are here Lucy, you too Chris." He says as he shakes Chris's hand before sitting back down and leaning his crutches against the table. "So Mum, Dad, what is it you wanted to say?" Callum gets straight to the point of our visit, I'm sure he is more desperate than any of us for answers.

But they don't say anything. Peter is looking at Callum and I together and it's like he is looking at a ghost, the bit of colour he had earlier has drained from his face. I know whatever they are about to say is bad. Possibly worse than anything I had imagined.

"I'm so sorry." He says, and it sounds like he is choking on his words "I just want you all to know how deeply sorry we are."

"What are you sorry for Dad?" Asks Sophie "I'm sure nothing can be that bad. Can it?"

Callum seems to be tired of waiting "If you want to tell me I'm adopted its fine Dad, I know you and Mum would have meant well, I'm starting to remember things already."

"What do you remember?" They cautiously ask together.

"Well, not much. I remember playing a lot with Lucy, then I remember things with Sophie, we played here in the fields as we were growing up. This house feels very familiar, I knew where my room was without being told, I knew the route here. I'm starting to see images of places and people, I recognise some faces from pictures on my phone and although I can't identify them yet, I remember a bit more of my life each day."

Peter takes a deep breath and looks at us all in turn before saying "I think it is important that we go back to the very beginning. This is going to be hard for Susan and I to say out loud, we've never actually spoken of some of this before so please just let me do this before you start jumping in with questions and so forth."

Susan is sitting with her head hanging down, shaking her head, her body is trembling as she tells Peter that she can't go through with it, she's so very sorry but it's just too hard. She looks like a broken woman as she holds tightly onto Peter's hand. He places his other hand on top and looks into her face softly as he tells her it is time for the truth to be told, she simply lowers her head with the slightest nod of agreement.

Chapter 25 Celeste

A few months after the party.

I'm pregnant. I've never been so scared. I don't know what to do. I'm being sick every morning and I think Brenda has noticed, she keeps trying to get me alone to talk but I keep avoiding her.

When I woke up the morning after my birthday party it was like the party had never happened, the house was tidy, Matt was at football training, and Martin and Brenda were happy after their night out, they even thanked me for keeping the house tidy while our friends had been here. I started to wonder if I had dreamed the whole experience with Matt, but unfortunately the pregnancy reminds me it is real. I missed a period which is nothing new, but then I missed another one so I bought a test. The lady in the chemist gave me a funny look as I was paying for it.

It's been a hard day at school, I was up earlier than usual being sick, and then we had a difficult maths assessment. Brenda is waiting for me when I get home from school, she demands to know what's going on. I tell her I'm fine but then she puts my pregnancy test down on the table in front of me. I had hidden it in my room, I'd planned to put into one of the bins at school so that nobody could find it and trace it back to me but I had been too scared, terrified that someone might see me, now I don't know why I hadn't wrapped it in something and got rid of it straight away to avoid this situation. Brenda's eyes are darting between the test and my face, I know there's no point in denying anything. It's almost a relief that somebody else knows, she might be able to help me.

I tell her the truth but she calls me a dirty little liar. I try to be strong but I fail, so I cry but she doesn't care. She tells me to get out of her sight, she says I am disgusting. I don't know who else to turn too or what to do so I just wander the streets until it gets dark, then I have no choice but to go home.

I find the three of them sitting around the kitchen table, they call me in to join them as soon as I close the front door. Martin tells me that he has contacted my social worker and I am to go back to the children's home. I tell them it is Matt's baby, he or she is their grandchild, but they call me a liar. Matt has denied everything; he won't even look at me.

Brenda goes off to make a phone call while we sit in an uncomfortable silence waiting for her to return. When she comes back she tells me I will be leaving their house within the next hour, the look she gives me is filled with hatred. I stand up to go to pack my things then realise that the filled bin bags I saw briefly when I passed through the hallway were my things.

We all sit in silence waiting for the time to come that I will leave. I try to look at Matt, to make him realise what he is doing but it's useless, he won't look at me. Every time Brenda looks at me she says something under her breath and shakes her head at me, her eyes narrowing each time.

I'm back in the children's home again, Karen has gone but I don't know where she went. The weeks are slowly ticking by while I exist in a land of misery and loneliness. I am almost six months pregnant now the doctor said, but if my life wasn't messed up enough already it gets worse, the doctor said I am having twins.

I don't go to school anymore, I walk and walk, there's nothing else to do. I have decided to have my babies adopted, everyone, all the official people that come to see me tell me it is the right thing to do. I have nothing to offer them, how can I offer my babies any kind of life when I can't even make my own life a success. When I unpacked my things the night I left Matt's house, I found an envelope of cash, there was a note in Martins writing telling me never to mention his sons name again, and I was to make sure I stayed away. I didn't really want his money but I wasn't strong enough to resist it, I use a little bit each day to buy a sandwich and a drink, then I sit by the river and think.

Today while I sat eating my lunch I met a nice man, he says he is called Wolf. I think I have seen him before, he said he has seen me here several times before. He asked why I always look so sad, so I told him my story. He said a baby is something to be thankful for, it's a miracle of nature. I think he is a bit crazy but he is funny and kind. He told me he has a friend who has inherited a big house, it's near the sea. He is going to go and stay with him, there will be lots of people there.

He says I could go with him and live in the big house too. I tell him I really don't think I could but he says I should think about it. He tells me nobody has to pay anything, we are all just going to help to make the old house nice again, he asks what skills I have, I think for a moment before I tell him that I can cook, I learnt some cookery skills from Brenda. He tells me if I want to go with him I should be back here by the river at the same time tomorrow, with my bag. I ask what I will do about my babies but he says there will be so many people to help me it will all be taken care of.

I didn't sleep last night, Wolfs suggestion kept going through my head. Could I really just disappear off to a new life without knowing much about it? But what's the alternative, I stay here, give up my babies, then carry on living my unimportant life. I've never had to make my own decisions before, I'm normally told what to do, whatever decision I make now won't just affect my life but those of my babies too.

By the time morning crept around I was ready, I had been ready for hours. I couldn't believe I was actually going to go through with it, but I was waiting by the river with my few possessions bundled into a bag. Wolf arrived on time making the whole ridiculous situation real, he was driving a funny looking campervan but seemed very happy to see me. He greeted me with a big smile then he picked me up and spun me around, then he took my bag from me and put it inside the van, as he opened the door for me I noticed a funny smell but I was too excited to care, I jumped into the van feeling a bubble of excitement brewing and waved goodbye to my old life.

Wolf said a new start needed a new name, he looked seriously at me with his head to the side, then he touched the gold necklace that I still always wore. I will call you Butterfly he said, so Celeste was gone and Butterlfy was born.

We drove nearly all day but we arrived just as it was getting dark and I was beginning to feel tired. The house that Wolf talked about was enormous, he introduced me to the people that he knew and we took a tour of the house, inside was not as nice as I had expected. Some of the rooms were very damp and it was sparsely furnished, I was given my own little bedroom and Wolf promised to help me to make it nice.

There were about twenty of us living there, although people came and went frequently. I gave birth to my babies very early one morning, just as the sun was coming up, Wolf found two other women to help me with the birth. Everyone was so kind to me, we took turns to look after each other's children. We worked in the gardens while the sun shone then we cooked and cleaned when it grew dark. Others worked on the roof, painted walls and fixed the rotting windows. There was always lots to eat and drink, and Wolf took good care of me and my babies, I had named them Lucy and Callum. Lucy had been my grandmother's name, I still carried the fond memories of our day to the beach from all those years ago.

The only problem was that I had discovered that the way Wolf made his money involved selling drugs, it caused a great many arguments between us. By now we were a couple, rather an odd couple really but it had just sort of happened slowly over a period of time.

Life was generally good, my children grew and were happy, they played with the other children at the house and one of the old ladies enjoyed spending time with the children. I had made friends and learnt a few skills from the other women, there were some girls my age and some were older, although ages didn't seem to matter here. The seasons changed and life rolled along, sometimes I had no idea what day it was or even which month we were in, nobody cared about such things.

The house was almost finished now; we had been here for just over three years. The man who owned it was going to sell it, this meant we all had to start making plans to move on, this worried me but Wolf said he had a plan. We would live in his campervan travelling place to place, working as we went. I wasn't sure about this because the children would soon need to go to school. He laughed at this and became angry, I didn't dare raise my concerns again. We did what he said, we lived on the road, he still made his money and although I didn't approve of how he did it I pretended not to know what was going on. Time after time I wanted to take my children and leave but I had no money and nowhere to go. I was trapped.

Chapter 26 Peter

"It was 1980, and I was seventeen years old, I had just had my birthday. My parents wanted me to go to university to get my degree and then go on to medical school to follow in my father's footsteps, the problem was that I always knew that wasn't the right career for me, I never wanted to be a doctor. I was more of an outdoors boy right from the time that I could walk. I was far more comfortable helping my grandparents out on their farm, I was happy in an old pair of Wellington boots mucking out the pigs or digging up potatoes.

I was much happier on the farm than I ever was at school, I detested pouring over books and writing essays, I wasn't any good at it either. My parents were horrified with my school reports and when I told them medical school definitely was not for me they were very angry, my father especially so, I had never seen him even half as angry as he was then. I told them I would like to study agriculture and they were both furious, so they issued me with an ultimatum.

Either I could follow the plans that they had made for my future as a doctor or I could move to the farm with my grandparents and stay there for good. If I chose the farm they said I would not be allowed back home, ever. It was an easy choice for me to make, I felt at home on the farm working on the land but I also thought that if they could cut me off so easily I obviously wasn't that important to them to begin with. So the next day I packed up the few personal belongings that I wanted to keep and said goodbye to my parents. My father didn't speak a word to me that morning and my mother gave me a brief kiss and said she was sorry. I boarded the train and came to live here on the farm with my grandparents. They were my father's parents.

My grandfather taught me all about the land and the animals, even how to predict the upcoming weather by looking at the sky, he knew so much about everything. Meanwhile, my grandmother taught me the basic things in life that my mother had never felt were important for me to know, she had called them women's jobs but my grandmother said it was important that I knew how to look after myself, she had always been quite an independent woman and believed there were no such things as men's jobs and women's jobs. My grandmother insisted that a farmer had to know how to cook a few basic meals for himself, how to wash clothes, and how keep a clean and tidy house. She was an amazing woman, actually, they were an amazing couple although my dad always insisted they had been terrible parents to him, I think deep down he was ashamed that his father was a farmer.

We lived and worked well alongside each other for eighteen months until tragedy struck and my grandfather suddenly died. He passed away peacefully in his sleep one night, it was a terrible time, my poor grandmother was understandably heartbroken and she passed away barely six months later. It was a truly awful time, I wrote to my parents after both deaths but I never had any response, they didn't even attend the funerals.

So, I was nineteen years old living alone with a farm to run, it was far from an easy time but I was determined to succeed, I couldn't let them down after they had believed in me, they had saved me from a life of doing what my father said regardless of my dreams.

Unfortunately though, I barely made enough money on the corn and the livestock to live on. I didn't know it when they were alive but my grandmother had inherited a vast sum of money in her youth which they had used carefully over the years to subsidise the farm. The last of the money in their bank account had paid for their funerals. I had to take the decision to sell off the remaining pigs and concentrate on the corn, I just hoped if they were looking down on me that they would understand.

About a year later I had a routine to my life and it was working out pretty well, it was a very simple life but I was content. I went to the local pub one night to treat myself to a pint because I had just completed the last harvest of the year. As I was thinking of leaving the door flew open and I was soaked head to toe by a girl shaking out her umbrella, I was momentarily furious but then I looked up and I was mesmerised the moment I saw her face. She had hair like polished walnut, rich and gleaming as she shook it out of her hat, her eyes were magical and full of promise. She had an energy about her and she seemed to light up the room, I couldn't stop thinking about her.

I went back to the pub the next week in the hope of seeing her again. There was a band playing that night so it was busy, then just as I thought she wasn't going to show she came in. I plucked up the courage and asked her to dance and I couldn't believe my luck when she said yes. She told me her name was Susan, we danced all night and that was when I knew she was the one for me. We married in the village church a year after our first meeting.

Those first few months were idyllic; we lived blissfully in our own little bubble. Susan knew and understood how important the farm was to me and she worked hard alongside me and turned the rambling old farm house into our home. I was happier than I ever imagined I could be. Susan always went to visit her Mum once a week but her health was deteriorating, her dad had left them years ago and had never made any contact since.

Unfortunately Susan's mother passed away just as we found out we were expecting Sophie. It was a sad time but we had to put our energy into getting ready for Sophie's arrival, the house was still a bit of a mess at that time, some of the rooms hadn't been used in years, we knew that life would be very different with a baby so we worked even harder to have everything ready for the baby's arrival.

During Susan's pregnancy she did all she could to help make the farm successful, then when Sophie was just twelve weeks old we found out that Susan was pregnant again. It was a shock we were not prepared for but we couldn't change fate. A healthy baby boy was born slightly earlier than we expected, we called him Jackson after my grandfather. The next few months were very hard for us with a dwindling farm and two children under a year old. We worked as hard as we could for as many hours a day that we had the strength for. Susan spent a lot of her time expanding her vegetable garden with Sophie and Jackson out there with her either sleeping in a pram or playing in a special pen I had built to keep them safe. The vegetables were selling extremely well at the local market and we were starting to make a little money.

We lived happily and content for a few years. We turned a field into a campsite and made a bit more money which was greatly needed with two rapidly growing children. Sophie and Jackson were both such happy little children, they had a strong bond between them which was lovely to see, Susan and I had both been only children and knew how lonely that could be. They sometimes played with other children that were staying on the campsite, we had a couple of families that worked in the orchards in exchange for a few nights on the site and some of the farms own eggs and vegetables, the children would often gather in the farmhouse kitchen for a cookie and a glass of milk in the afternoons. Life was good, we couldn't have been any happier.

Then one day early in September in 1988 Susan surprised me with a picnic lunch. Sophie and Jackson had helped to make cakes and little sandwiches, and had picked the last of the strawberries. We sat on a blanket under the big Oak tree in the bottom field and ate it all whilst laughing and chatting. We had been experimenting with cider recipes using our own apples, we were pretty sure this latest recipe was the best and the one we were going to produce along with our jam and chutneys. Susan and I had had a few glasses each and it was a warm sunny day so we had a lay down on the blanket and looked up to the sky, because that was one of the things we had always done, we liked to watch the clouds and the wind in the trees. We could hear Sophie and Jackson playing beside us on the rug.

I'm not sure how long for but we both fell asleep. I remember being woken by a piercing scream that sent shivers the length of my body. I woke Susan up and took her hand as I raced towards where I thought the scream had come from, I could hear Sophie now, and she was calling for her brother. I found her standing in a little clearing in the woodland. They had been told never to come in here because it was too was dangerous with all the brambles and dead trees. I had been meaning to clear the area and do something with it, maybe make it into a real nature reserve or a picnic area but there was never enough time.

Sophie explained how it was her turn to count but she had only got to eighteen or nineteen when she had heard her brother screaming. She had looked for him but couldn't see him. We worked our way out from where Sophie said he was, we didn't think he could have gone far in the time span and he was only small, Susan took Sophie with her and I went in the other direction to look for Jackson. Time stood still while we were calling for Jackson, I couldn't believe I had lost my little boy.

We searched everywhere, then I pushed my way around a broken horse chestnut tree, one of the branches was hanging over the path, I made my way through it, stamping the branches to the ground and tearing off handfuls of leaves in my haste to get through. Then I remember falling to the ground, I had to cover my eyes, I didn't want to see the sight of Jacksons little dumper truck sitting on the edge of the old well.

How I managed to persuade Susan to take Sophie home that day I will never know, there are fragments of that day that I still can't recall accurately. Once they had gone I looked deep into the well but could only see darkness. I went to the barn and got ropes and a torch and took them with me back to the well, checking in the bushes and calling for Jackson along the way, even though I knew it was hopeless.

I tied one end of the rope to a tree and lowered myself deep down into the well, there had once been a cover on the opening but over the years it had rusted away to dust. I lowered myself deeper and deeper down into the cold and dark, holding my breath until my feet eventually touched the bottom. I cautiously shone the torch around the base and then I realised that I was standing on Jacksons little shoe, his broken body was laying just inches away from me, his glassy eyes were looking directly at me. I bent down and gently closed his eyes as I fell to the ground beside him.

I don't know how long I stayed down there cradling the lifeless shell of my little boy but when I resurfaced it was dark. The night air was still around me and the stars were bright, I went back to the field and found the picnic blanket, then I lowered myself back into the well and wrapped Jackson's little body up in it.

When I got back to the farmhouse Susan had put Sophie to bed and she was staring into the flames of a fire. The orange and red flickers were almost hypnotising her. I told her I hadn't been able to find Jackson, I'm sure she didn't believe me but she silently wiped the tears from my face before they fell again and mingled with her own.

The next few days and weeks passed in a blur, I honestly can't tell you what we did. We kept out of the way of the last few campers. I vaguely remember telling a young woman she could stay as long as she wanted on the site if she picked the last of the apples.

It was about two weeks later that Susan came into the kitchen very early in the morning, she had taken to walking at odd hours, time and days meant nothing to us anymore. I remember it was early morning because the sun was just coming up and the grass was wet, shiny and slick with dew.

In her arms she had the body of a boy, he was filthy dirty and she had wrapped him in her cardigan. I thought for a moment she had found Jackson but how could that be, I knew where I had left him, she couldn't possibly have found our little boy. She sat down at the kitchen table gently rocking him in her arms, I couldn't speak, I didn't understand what I was seeing, but then slowly he opened his eyes.

He didn't know where he was or what had happened to him so Susan explained that she had been walking down by the river and she had found him, he was almost completely hidden by a bush, almost as though he had crawled under it for shelter. Her maternal instinct had kicked in and she had wrapped him up and bought him back home, he soon fell asleep and we just sat there. She gently rocked him in her arms as she sung softly to him, I really don't know what I was thinking or doing, I was drinking rather too heavily during that period in a bid to block out the pain of losing Jackson.

The radio was on in the background that morning telling us that late last night a campervan had been discovered following a collision with a tree, it looked like the occupants had been killed instantly, it was thought to be the parents of the boy who had drowned in the river earlier that same day. I remember hearing about a young boy who had gone missing from a field by a pub a few miles away. I had a feeling it was the campervan belonging to our apple pickers, I had noticed it driving down our lane earlier that afternoon or maybe it was the day before, as I said, I was drinking far too much to be able to construct any sensible thoughts. I remember she was a friendly young woman, pretty too. I don't think the man was the children's father but that was their business. She was very young and a bit of a hippy, she called herself Butterfly. She had been a good worker but totally unconventional. It was a shame if it was her family that had been killed, I'd liked the girl.

The boy woke again a while later, so we gave him something to eat and asked him his name. He couldn't remember, he had no memories at all, although he could ask for juice and he told us he was cold. I thought he looked vaguely familiar but I didn't know why. As the day wore on Sophie played with him and looked after him. She was four by then and was quite sensible so we left her playing with him.

I told Susan we should contact the police because someone would be looking for him, she said there was nothing on the radio about a missing boy so maybe he didn't belong to anyone. After two weeks of living in pure misery she was actually getting a little of her colour back. The boy was tired after several hours of playing with Sophie so we gave him a bath and put him to bed in one of the spare rooms. Sophie had still been asking frequently where Jackson was but the day the boy came she had asked less about Jackson. We never did admit that Jackson had died, not to ourselves or to anyone. We always told Sophie she would see him later, or that he was unwell so he was sleeping when she had asked.

I'm honestly not sure how this came to happen but as the days wore on the boy stayed with us, he still had no memories but was happy playing in his room or looking at books, we kept Sophie away if we could so she didn't ask too many questions or tire him too much, he was a very fragile little boy. Sophie was at school now so she was gone during part of the day. I walked her to and from school each day carefully avoiding everyone else. The headmistress caught me one day and asked where Jackson was, I'd forgotten he had been due to start nursery, I could feel my eyes welling up as I told her that he had been very unwell and he was still quite fragile.

As the weeks wore on the boy gained some weight and looked very well, he began to play in the garden with Sophie in the afternoons. We had started dressing him in some of Jackson's clothes and as much as I didn't want too I started to care for the boy. I still visited Jackson every single day to say a prayer, I think Susan was living in a daze during this period, I'm not sure if she ever acknowledged that the boy wasn't truly hers.

One afternoon in early December we were eating dinner when Sophie called the boy Jackson, Susan and I both froze at that point but he asked if that was his name, we couldn't bring ourselves to answer him but Sophie said of course it was, so from that day onwards the boy, Callum, became Jack. We could never call him Jackson and Sophie was forbidden to call him that.

Susan never to this day has asked what I had found that day when Jackson disappeared. We have never spoken to anyone of the arrival of Jack. Until now."

Chapter 27 Celeste

Today Lucy and Callum are four. Wolf gave me some money so I could get them a birthday badge each and a cake, Lucy wanted a balloon too, one of those shiny ones that float in the sky. We have been camping on a beautiful little site, our money is running low although Wolf says that's about to change, the farmer has let us stay for free if we pick his apples, its hard work but I enjoy it, the children play on the site with some other children while I work, Wolf goes off by himself, sometimes he comes back very drunk, that's when his temper can flare.

This morning Lucy got upset, she accidentally left a toy on the floor, Wolf tripped over it and he almost fell over, I told her it didn't matter, everything was okay, but Wolf shouted at her, then he trampled on her toy and made her pick up all of the tiny broken pieces. I'm working on our escape. I keep thinking about calling Emma, to ask for her help.

We had to go to the pub to meet some of Wolf's friends, lots of packages and money changed hands under the table. The children have gone to play in the field next to us, I don't like them being around Wolfs friends, their language is horrible. I am watching Callum chase his ball while Lucy makes daisy chains.

Suddenly I can't see Callum, but I can hear Lucy screaming. I realise that Callum is in the river, I run frantically through the field towards the river, trying to get to my little boy, I watch helplessly from the bank as he is swept away, an older boy is standing with Lucy. I shout to Wolf to call for help, police or ambulance, somebody has to help me. He says he can't call the police until he has hidden his stash. He and his mates disappear. The lady in the pub calls the emergency services and waits with me and Lucy for them to arrive. I want to jump in the river after Callum but a big man holds me back saying it's too dangerous, I just want to get to my little boy.

Police come and search the river banks for miles around while diving teams search the river, it grows dark and still Callum hasn't been found. My heart feels like it is breaking into millions of tiny pieces. Wolf comes back for us just as the police say they can't do anymore until first light. Wolf ignores my cries to stay here, he puts me and Lucy in the van in slams the door shut behind us.

When he starts to drive away I tell him to stop. We will stay here and wait for the police to come back in the morning. He gets very angry and says he isn't going anywhere near any police and he starts to drive off. I try to make him stop but he won't listen to me, he is shaking my shoulders and hitting me on the head, the pain he is inflicting doesn't even come close to the pain of losing my baby boy.

Up ahead I can see a tree, illuminated by the moonlight, we are travelling too quickly towards it, I brace myself as the scream leaves my lips.

Chapter 28 Jack/Callum

The coffee sits untouched on the table, it has long since grown cold but nobody has noticed. The silence drags out and still nobody speaks. Dad looks as though he is expecting a response from each of us, he is looking around the table at each of us in turn, his eyes come back to rest on me. I was expecting to be told that I was adopted, I had got used to that idea, but this, this is unbelievable, but yet it must be true.

"You stole me." I say in a barely audible voice. "If Lucy hadn't have found me would you ever have told me the truth?"

Dad is shaking his head when my mum tells me that I am her son, she may not have given birth to me but she's watched me grow into the brilliant man she says I am today, she reminds me that she has nursed me through chicken pox and ear infections, she's helped me with my homework and she's cared for me and supported me through every step I have made. She says she couldn't have loved me more.

"But you've both lied to be every day of my life; you called me Jack knowing that I was probably the missing boy Callum."

"You are absolutely right son." Sighs Peter "But we couldn't be sure who you were and I told myself that even if you were the boy that had supposedly drowned your parents had had that terrible accident and been killed, so you see, you needed someone to look after you, and we were the ones that did that."

"But as I got older did you think I would ever find out, or maybe wonder if I deserved to know the truth?"

"The truth is, your mother and I thought of you as ours."

"But you took a three year old boy and passed him off as your dead son, do you have any idea how messed up that is?" I know I'm shouting now but I can't help it, the shock of finding out who I really am has bought all of my frustration and anger of the accident back to the surface again, I feel like my life is totally out of control, I don't know if anything I thought I knew is real.

"Jack," Says my mum "I can't change the past, we really didn't think clearly about what we were doing, by the time the fog had started to clear in my head and I had accepted that Jackson had died you were so much a part of our family, I loved you."

"It's just a lot for me to take in; my whole life has been one big lie."

"There is just one more thing you should probably know." My mum says and she leaves the room, returning just a few moments later with a box, it's white with faded blue stripes, like the kind you put a present in. She puts the box down on the table in front of me and indicates I should open it. Inside is a little pair of denim shorts, I put those on the table and pull out a badge.

"That was in your pocket." She tells me. I'm holding a little birthday badge, it's a rainbow on a blue background and under the rainbow is a number four. I silently pass it to Lucy.

"But I was told I was three, were we were actually four?" Lucy is asking. I'm not sure who she is asking but my mum nods her head. It seems you were four but Jack was so small, he was half the size of Sophie who was four. He just slipped into the hole that Jackson had left, he had been three so therefore Jack became three.

Lucy is holding the badge, turning it over in her hand. "We had a rainbow cake, do you remember it Callum?"

"I think I do. We blew the candles out together." He says smiling.

"We did, I remember it too. I think we did everything together." Lucy tells me.

"Is there anything else I should know?" I ask my parents.

Together, my parents, if that's what I still call them, shake their heads and the room falls silent again.

"I have a question." Says Sophie who has been sitting quietly. "Where is my brother, where is Jackson?"

"Follow me." Says my dad. "Put your coats on, it will be cold out there." So silently we wrap up warm and cautiously make our way outside. We are all wondering what will happen next.

Sophie

Jack is standing with his good arm wrapped around Carrie, he looks shattered. Lucy and Chris are standing waiting awkwardly next to Josh and I. Lucy has confided that she thinks her and Chris should go home, she feels they are intruding on a family issue that she isn't part of, I tell her that as we all seem to be connected in one way or another I would like her to stay, so she agreed.

Dad leads the way across the driveway and off across the garden, mum is reluctantly following at a distance. We pass the slightly neglected vegetable garden and then climb over an old wobbly wooden style and walk down a slippery path that takes us to the field. The old oak tree stands stark and bare taking ownership of the field, as we pass it mum stops and touches the trunk of the tree, possibly remembering happier times, or maybe just to steady herself. Dad slows and waits for her, looping his arm through hers, offering her support.

At the bottom end of the field is a wooden fence that looks like it was put up long ago as it's now covered in ivy and blackberry bushes. Dad clearly knows what he is looking for as he grabs hold of a padlock that wouldn't be easily visible, he slides the key from his pocket and cautiously unlocks the gate, nobody seems to want to go through first, we all seem to be rooted to the spot. Then Lucy boldly, or impatiently, makes the first move to step through and everyone else follows while Dad closes the gate softly behind us.

"It's beautiful." Says Lucy, and she is right. We seem to have entered an oasis for wildlife. Underneath the canopy of trees hang bird feeders and little wooden bird houses are nestled in the trees. As we walk on along the path there is a pond that I imagine is home to an assortment of creatures. There are small wooden boxes dotted about the woodland floor that dad says are hedgehog houses.

As we walk I'm taking in my surroundings, it's like we have entered another land, I'm reminded of the secret garden which was one of my childhood favourites, Then too soon we come to a stop, I can see a small stone wall, its angular grey bricks are arranged to form a circular shape. As I get closer and we stand arched around it I realise it is a well. It has been covered over with planks of aging wood and a marble angel sits on top.

"You left him in there?" Shrieks my mum.

Dad looks panicked so Jack wraps his good arm tightly around mum while I'm frozen to the spot, I can't take my eyes off the angel.

"Is my brother in there, in that well?"

Dad doesn't speak but he nods and hangs his head, a few moments pass then he tells us "Yes, Jackson is in there. I thought about moving him but I couldn't do it, it was almost as though he had chosen this spot. I thought he would be safe down there."

I noticed a few snowdrops beginning to bloom earlier so I go back to pick them and then I place them carefully under the shadow of the angels wings. We stand there silently for a few minutes, I'm finding today is much harder than anything I had expected. I never imagined events of the past could unsettle me so much, I notice my mum is quietly crying while dad tries, and fails, to comfort her.

Carrie and Chris are sitting a little way away on a bench by the pond so Josh and I go and sit with them,

"Where have Jack and Lucy gone?" I ask.

Carrie tells me Jack said he needed a bit of space, he is having trouble separating his memories from his flashback dreams, he isn't sure which are Callum's or Jack's memories so Lucy followed him out, she didn't want him to be alone.

Lucy

I find Callum sitting awkwardly on a log under the shelter of the old oak tree so I sit down beside him.

"I've never been in this field before, dad told me and Sophie years ago that it wasn't our land so I was never to set foot in here, now I know why."

"Callum, I'm so sorry about all of this, if I had never of come looking for you then you would be so much happier now, so would Sophie, she wouldn't have had to go through all this.

"No Lucy, you are so wrong, If you hadn't have found me I wouldn't have been any happier, it's true that my memories are coming back a few more each day and hopefully I will remember everything, but in the hospital as soon as the nurse mentioned my sister my first thought was of you, I said my sister is Lucy, I had remembered you. I have been doing some reading into it, Carrie has been helping, it seems it took me losing my memory again to help me to unlock the memories that I had lost previously. So if you hadn't of tracked me down to the hospital it would only have been a matter of time until I would have come looking for you."

We talk about what happens next, who will he decide to be? I am not surprised when he tells me he doesn't have a choice, he has to be Jack. Practically it makes sense, his life is in Jacks name, his bank account, driving licence, qualifications, everything. He tells me he feels like he has lived two lives, he had his few years as Callum but he stopped being Callum when he went into the river. He has spent the majority of his life as Jack so feels it is important to move forward as Jack.

Then I ask him if he has thought about reporting his parents for what they did. He takes a while to answer but when he does he says he can't even think about that at the moment, which I try to understand. I think part of me wants Peter and Susan to pay for taking my brother from me though. I look up and see that the others are coming over, I pull Callum to his feet and he gives me a hug. We all walk back up to the farm house together, fighting against the icy wind and shivering in the cold.

Susan tells us all to go through to the lounge where Peter has put another log onto the fire. She brings through a pot of tea and a large homemade fruit cake, I can see how well she has looked after my brother and I will understand it if he feels its best just to let the past go.

We are all hungrier than expected and the cake is soon gone. Peter asks if there is anything else any of us want to ask, as he does this he fetches a bottle of whisky from a cupboard in the corner and fills a selection of glasses although it's not even lunchtime yet. I catch the look between Sophie and Callum and then Sophie asks,

"The locked room upstairs, was that Jackson's room?"

"Yes, it will always be Jackson's room." Susan tells them sadly.

"Can I please go in there Mum?" Asks Sophie.

Susan looks like she is about to refuse then she seems to change her mind as she nods and slowly reveals a necklace that's been tucked into her jumper, on the necklace is a small bronze key.

Chapter 29 Sophie

As I follow Mum up the stairs I am almost regretting asking to do this, it's just the two of us now but I can almost feel Jackson's presence, more so as she turns the key in the lock and we enter his room. I'm not sure what I expected to find, dust and stale air maybe, but the sight before me is nothing like that. Piled up next to his bed are towers of presents and there is a box that is almost full to the brim with cards.

"Mum?" I say, I can't take my eyes of all this. She tells me she has bought him a birthday and Christmas present every year without fail since he disappeared, she had always refused to believe that he was dead; she was waiting for him to come home. I cross the room and wrap her in my arms while she sobs.

My eyes are combing every inch of the room, taking in everything that I had forgotten about. The toy chest filled with building blocks and tiny toy cars that sit in the corner of the room tucked under the eaves, the grey rocking horse that stands by the window, Jackson called him Neddy. But most of all I remember how much he loved his little trucks, they are still sitting in rows on his floor. Mum must move them to clean and then put them back in exactly the same spot, the room is immaculate, it's evident she spends a lot of time in here keeping it as it was that last day, which is just simply heartbreaking.

I can't take my eyes of the framed photo that hangs on the wall, it was taken in front of the Christmas tree, Jackson is smiling into the camera and holding a big wrapped present in his little hands, he has brown curls several shades lighter than mine and we share the same hazel eyes. It must have been taken the year before he died, his last Christmas. I'm ashamed to admit I had forgotten what the real Jackson looked like but now I can see him I can remember him clearly, looking back at the photo now I feel a great sense of pain and sorrow.

Although I know now that I lost him years ago that day in 1988 it feels raw, as far as I knew my brother was alive, I wasn't given anytime to grieve for him, I was just given a replacement. I do empathise with my parents' situation but I also feel so angry with them, how dare they let me believe my brother was alive for all these years. I'm not sure if I can ever forgive them for what they have done but then I do also understand that grief can make you do things your rational mind wouldn't normally contemplate.

We take our time, breathing in everything of Jacksons. I almost feel like a little girl again, like I've come in here to take him off to play something outside, he always used to play any game I wanted. He knew hide and seek was my favourite, that's why he wanted to play it that day, he had wanted me to teach him to count properly and we had spent lots of time practising because he wanted to count like I could .

When we leave Jacksons room to go back down mum goes to lock the door then sighs as she realises that there are no secrets to lock away anymore, she still tucks the little key back into her jumper and I watch her hold the key to her chest before she goes down the stairs.

When we are back down with the others we find everyone is drinking my dad's whisky in an effort to warm up. The fire is doing its best but I think we are all just numb. Mum disappears into the kitchen and I sense its best to let her be alone for a while. Lucy is asking my dad what he remembers of her mother, he doesn't remember much, only that she seemed far too young to have left home and had children. She picked apples in exchange for a free pitch, and that was it really. He thinks the man with her was called Wolf or something, definitely an animal name, very strange for a man that age, he was a very big, intimidating man, possibly about forty. Then Callum remembers the man called Wolf used to call him Cub, and Lucy was called kitten. The past is slowly coming back to us, a few trickles of a memory triggers another fragment of someone else's memory.

Mum comes back telling us that there is soup on the stove and fresh bread if we are hungry. Surprisingly we find we are all ravenous. When we finish eating dad cautiously asks Jack if he has made any decisions about what happens next. Jack looks thoughtful for a while before he tells them he doesn't think there is anything to gain by bringing the police into this, if they were charged and put in prison it wouldn't change what has already happened, they had been good parents to him and were clearly still devastated by the loss of Jackson. He said there was me to consider too, he didn't think I deserved to lose my parents, or for Daisy to lose her grandparents.

All the time that I'm listening to Jack talking I feel like I am at the table with a stranger, which is crazy because I've grown up with him. The truth is it is going to take time to adjust to this new situation, I know our bond is strong, but it's not like the bond he shares with Lucy. I'm scared I will lose another brother.

The relief on my parent's faces when Jack says he won't go to the police is evident but there is sorrow there too. Maybe they are wondering if they did the right thing in telling us the truth after all these years. Then I ask something I have been thinking all morning.

"Was what happened to Jackson the reason why you both became so distant with me, and with the rest of the world?"

"Oh Sophie, we were so scared someone would find out that Jack wasn't ours, at the beginning we just had to shut ourselves away, I know it meant you missed out on things, I realised later that we never encouraged you to have friends over to stay and we never had any parties or anything, we just tried to keep our lives as private as we could. I think we did temporarily distance ourselves from you because it was just so painful when you wouldn't stop asking for Jackson, I really am truly sorry, we loved you deeply but we were lost in our grief, we didn't consider how much you were missing him too. That's why when you called Callum Jack it was just so easy to let it be. As the years passed it became easier to hide away, we grew as much of our own food as possible, we burned our own fuel and lived a very simple life, we had lost touch with our old friends and we didn't seek out any other company, I think we almost forgot what it was like to be with other people. It was always easier to visit you rather than have you here because we didn't want you to see us living like that. It's funny because as strange as it seems under the circumstances it's been really nice to have some company here today."

Chapter 30 Lucy

Susan brings out more food and we stay sat around the table in the warmth of the kitchen and talk. Susan asks about my adoptive parents, asking if I had a good upbringing, she feels she should have looked out for us more when we were here, she wondered if my mum was coping okay and the man didn't seem very nice, she tells me she thinks she remembers Callum, although she calls him Jack, and I playing with Sophie and Jackson on a few afternoons just after we had arrived, that was when my mum was a paying customer, she stayed for a few weeks before her money ran out then Susan thinks that's when the man came too and she started picking the apples in order to stay.

Susan tells me that while my mum worked in the orchards she would sing along to the pop music that she was listening too, they always knew where she was because she never stopped singing, I can remember lots of singing too. I think I have so many memories locked away in the back of my mind but all it takes is a gentle nudge to free them, I can almost hear her singing now if I close my eyes and take myself back through the years.

I'm grateful to Susan for sharing these memories with me it's good to know we were a happy little family at some point in time. I ask her about the river, the one that I saw Callum taken away in. She tells me it was just a mile or so away through the fields, longer by road. The pub is next to the field we had been playing in. She offers to take me but I don't think that's necessary today.

"Lucy," Callum says "I would like to see it; I think it would help me if you would come back there with me, it won't be dark for another hour, can we go, please?"

I'm not sure that it is a good idea to go back there on top of everything else today but I can't bring myself to say no to Callum. Chris offers to drive us there and Susan gives him the details.

It doesn't take long to reach the pub, The Peacock is an old white building, with visible beams, and snowdrops are growing in clusters on the grass by the entrance. As we pull into the car park the untreated snow that is crunching beneath us isn't enough to distract me from the frantic pounding in my ears, I feel uncomfortable being back here, the place that changed my life. Then I remind myself that however anxious I'm feeling Callum must be feeling a hundred times worse. He climbs out of the car first and waits for me to follow, I feel like I'm glued to the spot but Chris tells me I have to be strong for Callum, I know he is right but the familiar fears are back with me. Slowly I unplug my seat belt, open the door, and step out of the car.

The snow is still clinging to the grass in patches but the ground is firm and easy to walk on. Callum gives my hand a squeeze then he holds tightly onto his crutches then together we walk across the field towards the river. The landscape looks bleak, the sky feels like it is closing in on us, wrapping us tightly in a cold dull blanket, the river is casting its evil spell, drawing us closer, its beauty camouflaging its deadly intent. I start to slow, then I stop a few steps back from the edge of the water but Callum hobbles forwards.

"Callum, please, that's close enough." I don't like him going so close, we know the dangers that this river possesses.

"I'm fine Lucy, I promise." Then leans forward and looks deep into the river. I don't want to be here any longer but Callum shows no sign that he is uncomfortable, he is actually smiling as he tells me he is remembering, but then his smile turns to something far worse.

Chapter 31 Callum age 4

"Please Mummy, will you come and play with me?"

"Not now, will you just go away boy." Snarls the nasty man.

"I want my mummy, not you." I tell him but then I shrink back because he looks angry, he scares us when he gets angry.

Then my mummy leaves the table and comes over and I really think she might come and play with me, she kneels down on the ground next to me to give me a cuddle, her hair tickles the side of my face making me giggle, then she tells me she loves me very much but she can't play now. She has to stay with the man we call Wolf. She says she has to stay with him and his friends for a little bit longer to keep him happy because she doesn't want him to get cross again. Nobody wants him cross again because we all remember what happens when he gets cross; he even makes my mummy cry sometimes.

She tells me that Lucy is playing with the flowers in the field next to us, she points to Lucy so I can see, and I nod even though I already know where Lucy is. The man is looking at me again with his cross looking eyes, they are small and black, like hard little stones buried in his face, then he throws a red football at me and says in a growl "Off you go boy." So with a last pleading look at my mummy I turn around and I go, I'm walking slowly because I don't want to leave my mummy with that nasty man.

I take my ball to the field where Lucy is sitting playing with the flowers at the edge of the field, she does this thing where she puts them together and wears it as a necklace, she made me one once but it smelled funny so I took it off and hung it on a tree but then she was cross with me, everybody gets cross with me but I just want to play.

I show Lucy my ball and ask her if she wants to play, she says she just needs a few more flowers to finish her necklace and then she will play with me. I'm so happy she said yes that I run off to get her some more of the smelly flowers then she can play with me sooner. I take my ball too because I must look after it extra well because he gets cross if we lose things. I kick it and then look for Lucy's flowers as I go to collect the ball, I can see it easily against the bright green grass. I do the game two times and I think I will just do it one more time then there should be enough flowers for Lucy.

As I kick the ball this last time the wind grabs hold of it and moves it further away from me, I'm running as fast as I can but the wind is faster than me, I can't catch my ball and I'm getting scared because I'm getting near to the river and mummy said not to go too close to the water.

My ball has landed on the edge of the river so I think I can reach it, but then just as I get close to it the wind makes it move again, now it is in the middle of the river. Wolf man scares me a lot so I have to get his ball back, I paddle out into the water, it's really cold.

The water starts to move very quickly and my ball is disappearing, I scream out as the water makes me fall over, I can see Lucy coming nearer. Then the water is taking me away, I can't stand up, my feet keep getting knocked over. My face is under the water now and I am more scared than ever before, even more scared than when Wolf got angry when I accidentally knocked his drink over. Now I feel like I am falling asleep, my body feels strange, a bit floppy and very cold, I worry that I can't hear Lucy anymore, I think I'm falling asleep.

Its dark now, the rain is falling so hard that it's difficult to see what's in front of me, the wind increases the force of the raindrops, stabbing my skin. I open my eyes and I don't know where I am, my body is aching and I am so very tired. I drag myself away from the edge of the river and tuck myself away under a bush, trying to shelter from the rain. I don't understand what has happened, my thoughts have all gone. I think I can hear shouting, it scares me so I move further under the bush, then I fall into a deep sleep.

I tell Lucy all that I have just remembered; she wraps her arms around me and rests her head on my shoulder. I hold onto her while I talk.

"Our fate was in the power of the river that day, this river had the power to change our lives in an instant, and it could have all been so different. If I hadn't of gone into the water that day we would have grown up together, Wolf would have been cross about the ball but we would have all gone back to the campsite that afternoon and everything would have been okay, we would have stayed together. It's entirely my fault Lucy, I'm so sorry, it's my fault that Mum died."

"No Callum, please don't say that. It was a terrible, terrible accident. Fate stepped in that day and ripped us apart, please don't blame yourself for this, we were just children, we were left alone to play in a meadow by the river, and as you said, our fate was in the hands of the river, we had no control over anything that happened that day."

"But if I had of stayed in the field with you where I was supposed to be ....." I find I am too emotional to finish. Despite what Lucy is saying I know it was entirely my fault.

"Please don't Callum, I know what you are thinking, what I don't understand is why nobody was watching us closer, I would never let Jasmine and Harrison that far out of my sight."

"I'm looking forward to meeting them both, hopefully one day soon."

"They are going to absolutely love you. Now, we need to stop looking into the past and instead we are going to look forward to the future, we've got so many lost years to make up for. I want to spend my time with you building new, happy memories. We can't change the past, no matter how much we would like to, but we can build a future. So, let's make a deal, no more what-ifs, just live our lives in the here and now, okay?"

"You've got yourself a deal. Now, let's go back to the car before it's too dark to find our way out of this field."

Chapter 32 Lucy

We walk back to the car slowly, Callum hobbling along on his crutches, we are both freezing cold and the biting wind had seeped deep into our bones. We absorb the warmth of the car, grateful that Chris has kept the heating running, he tells me he has spoken to my mother and the children are both fine, they have been having a great time baking cookies.

Callum sits silently on the back seat during the journey back, he is rubbing his head, I wonder if he is willing all of his memories to return, or maybe he is trying to rub the pain of the past away.

We go back to the farm house where Sophie and the others are waiting eagerly for any more news on Callum's memory, I'm starting to feel less like an intruder in this house now, as we enter Chris hangs our coats on chairs in front of the fire. Callum shares with them what he has just remembered but he looks exhausted as he finishes his recount. As the day wears on we end up sitting at the table talking about our lives and drinking Peter's whisky, we don't notice as it grows dark outside.

When I notice the time I whisper to Chris that we should be going but Peter overhears and points out that it is now snowing so hard it would be best to wait until morning, he assures us they have plenty of room and we must all stay the night, I'm not sure I feel comfortable with staying here but as Chris points out we have both had a couple of whisky's, so we agree to stay. We were planning to stay at a little hotel a few miles away but Susan goes off to light fires in the spare rooms which probably haven't been used in decades given their chosen lifestyle. Peter tops up all of our glasses although Carrie still hasn't touched hers and he throws another log onto the dying fire.

Peter sits back in his chair with a contented sigh as he swirls the amber liquid in his glass and inhales the aroma. I realise that although today must have been quite an ordeal for Peter and Susan, he looks like the weight has begun to leave his shoulders, keeping secrets like he has done was a heavy load to bear.

He asks about our children so while I'm chatting Chris takes out his phone and shows Peter some pictures. Sophie says she's sure Daisy would like to meet Jasmine and Harrison, after all, they are almost cousins, that make us all laugh. Carrie asks lots of questions about having children; I almost feel she is taking notes. Susan comes back down and looks over Peter's shoulder, he is looking at a picture of Harrison from last summer, it was taken in our garden where he is playing with dinosaurs in his sandpit, his golden curls a halo in the sunshine.

"Oh my goodness." She exclaims, that looks just like Jack did when he came to us." So I tell her about Harrison, and how looking at Harrison had felt familiar, it had triggered something deep inside me and had helped to unlock my memories of Callum.

Susan tells me she would like to get to know us better, as we are clearly part of Jack's life now she would like to include us in her family, it's a very strange feeling but I can see what she means. It's such an unusual situation for all of us; it feels like we are making up the rules as we go along. Peter is enthused by the idea of spending more time together because he starts talking about how much fun the children could have collecting eggs from their chickens and playing with Daisy in the garden. I get the sense that both Peter and Susan have been lonely for a very long time. I sense that deep down they are good people but I can't begin to forgive them yet for depriving me of all of those lost years without my brother.

More whisky is poured and Susan feeds us cold meat and cheese while more tales are told from Jackson and Sophie's childhood. Callum is curiously quiet but he's had an extraordinary day of revelations to deal with. I lean into Chris feeling sleepy but oddly content. It is a relief to know I wasn't imagining or hallucinating any of those episodes, I feel stronger now that I know I was right.

Jack/Callum

My mind won't stop churning; it's been such a roller coaster of a day there's just so much to think about. I'm lying on the bottom bunk in my childhood bedroom staring into the darkness; I used to sleep on the top one but with my leg still in plaster I couldn't get up there. Carrie is sleeping peacefully in the bunk above me but I'm too restless to sleep.

I am Callum and I am Jack, the problem is I don't feel like I am either of them. It sounds like Callum came from a pretty dysfunctional family, and I honestly think if I hadn't have gone into the river that day I would have lead a very different life entirely, a life living on the road in a van, I can't see that would have lead to a great shot at an education. Or, maybe their fate was always to crash that night, maybe if I hadn't have gone missing I might have been killed in that crash, and Lucy as well.

I wake up swimming in a pool of sweat, I dreamt that I was in the van when it crashed, I could see myself covered in blood. I try to shake the nightmare from my head and as I do so my memories are rushing back, my head feels like it is going to explode. I slip out of bed as quietly as I can, I'm dressed in sweatpants and a hoodie because I remember how cold this house gets at night, I reach into the wardrobe to pull a fleece top on as well.

"Jack, are you okay? What's happening?"

"Sorry Caz, I didn't mean to wake you." And then she's leaping up out of bed throwing her arms around me.

"What's all this for?" I ask her, she looks so happy considering it's the middle of the night and I've just woken her up.

"Jack, you called me Caz, that's what you always called me before, I didn't tell you about that so that means you've remembered."

"Yes, I think I have. I can remember lots about you now." And I kiss her, I notice she is crying but she says they are happy tears, she clings onto me, burying her face in my shoulder, I can't believe I ever forgot her, she is the most amazing woman I have ever met. I reach back into my wardrobe and find her something warm to wear, she doesn't question what I'm thinking, she dresses quickly, shivering against the cold, and then quietly we leave the room together, giggling like a pair of teenagers.

We grab a couple of old wax jackets from the utility room and go outside, I felt too claustrophobic in the house. As we walk I tell Carrie how my memories came rushing back after that terrible dream. I can remember the first time I met her, how she changed my life. I can remember my time at university, with Josh and Sophie. I can remember that on Christmas Eve I had been thinking about her, missing her more than I thought humanly possible, then I remember that I left all of my Christmas shopping under the table in the pub.

Then I tell her that I think my parents saved me, I honestly think they gave me a better life than I would otherwise have had, now I feel like I would like to do something for them. I can vividly remember how much I dislike my job, as we walk around the farm in the shadow of the moonlight we talk about the things we could do with this farm if we were given the chance. Carrie says she has always dreamt of having her own little tea shop, living in the countryside with her family. We talk for hours, making plans for our future and catching up on lost time until the sun slowly begins to rise.

Chapter 33 Lucy

It feels as though my head has only just hit the pillow when I peel my eyes open to look at the time on my phone, I'm shocked to see that its almost eight o'clock. I've slept for an amazing ten straight hours. I ease myself up and perch on the side of the bed, the fire has gone out and the room is freezing. I don't know why Peter and Susan haven't had central heating installed, they rely solely on the warmth of the fires. I gently nudge Chris to wake him up, I really want to get going as early as possible. We need to go home and pick up our things to take to my parent's house, so as tempting as it is to fall back into bed I force myself to brace the cold and head for the even colder bathroom. I have the quickest shower I've ever had and when I'm done I wake Chris up again, making sure to do it properly this time.

"Hey, surely it's not morning, it's still almost dark." Chris croaks from beneath the blankets, we had sheets and real old fashioned blankets, not a duvet which was a bit odd at first but then once I was used to it the weight of the blankets felt reassuring, I slept better than I have in a long time. Chris is right about it being dark though, I open the curtains and gaze outside at the darkness surrounding us, with no other houses nearby and no street lights it's like another world. Suddenly I sense movement and I turn around to see Chris is throwing the pile of blankets back and sitting bolt upright, then a second later he is pulling his clothes on.

"What's going on?" I ask him, I can't believe he is suddenly moving so quickly.

"Smell the air Lucy, what do you smell?"

I think he has gone crazy but then I smell it too, the delicious smell of bacon is wafting into our room. We follow the tantalizing smell across the landing and downstairs into the kitchen where we find Peter cooking up the biggest pan of bacon and fried eggs I have ever seen. He stops whistling when he sees us.

"Good morning, there's tea and toast over there on the table, get started on that and I'll bring this lot over in a moment." Then he resumes his happy whistling. So we do as we were told to do, Susan joins us with Sophie and Josh so together we eat piles of eggs and bacon washed down with mugs of the strongest tea imaginable. Just as I'm wondering where Callum is he and Carrie stumble into the room arm in arm looking incredibly happy, they are wrapped in hats and coats and they are giving off cold air after an early morning walk.

"It's nearly all back; I've been awake almost all night." Callum says "I even remember everything about my job and how much I hated it, I can't believe I ever thought being an accountant was a good idea!"

"So what kind of job would you like to do?" I ask him between mouthfuls of food.

"Well, I've given that a bit of thought over the last few hours and I think, well if it is okay with mum and dad, I would like to do something agricultural, I loved growing up here on the farm and I just think there is so much wasted potential. Now that all the secrets are out in the open there's no need to hide ourselves away, I'll continue with the accountant thing because looking at my bank balance it seems to pay quite well, but I was wondering, Mum, Dad, if you would let me try to do something here with you on the farm?"

"What do you mean by try something?" Peter asks, although I can see he is intrigued, he takes another slice of bacon as he sits back and listens.

"I've got no idea at the moment Dad but I feel it's something I want to do, I feel happy here, I want to help make a real success of this place, if you'll let me?"

"Well then son, that sounds like a good idea. You get your ideas together and then we can start to make a plan."

"Carrie dear, how do you feel about this, would you be happy if Jack spent more time here?" Asks Susan cautiously.

"It's something I hadn't considered before now but I have to admit I understand his thinking. You have so much land here and Jack is right, there is a lot of potential, you could have a tea room and a shop selling your own produce, even animals for the children to look at and feed. It's great to see Jack so excited about something, and I could help too, if you would let me."

"Oh, and the other thing," Jack says looking to Carrie for her approval; she nods so he carries on "I'm going to be a dad, Carrie is pregnant, she told me last night."

"Well then son, if you are both serious about taking on this farm, and transforming it into something to be proud of, how about you build yourselves a home in one of the empty fields, then you can raise your children out here in the country, what do you think?"

"Wow, that's quite an offer Dad, what do you think Mum?"

"I think that's the best idea your dad has ever had." And there are tears in her eyes.

Carrie is nodding eagerly along to their plans, she looks radiantly happy, a total transformation from the day I first met her just barely two weeks ago in the hospital. There are hugs and congratulations all round. Then it hits me, I'm going to be an aunt. I've got my brother back and I'm going to have a niece or nephew too. It really has been a busy few days full of revelations. We eat another plate of eggs and bacon washed down with more tea before we manage to leave the table. I go back up to our room to make sure we have everything we came with which admittedly wasn't much. I'm eager to get going to see Jasmine and Harrison and I know mum and dad will be desperate to know the story of what happened to Callum.

As we are about to leave I realise that I haven't seen Sophie for a while so I go to look for her to say goodbye. I make my way along the upstairs corridor and I hear her through a crack in the door. I tap lightly before entering; I find her sitting in the window seat crying.

I pick up the tissues from next to the bed and hand them to her. I tell her we are about to leave and thank her for including us yesterday. She shrugs her shoulders and says through her sobs "Well you are his sister, not me." Then I realise why she is upset. I sit down next to her and she moves over to give me some space.

"Sophie, I know all of this has been a terrible shock for you, I can't pretend to understand how you must be feeling, to know you lost your brother all of those years ago must be simply awful, but remember I do know a bit about what it's like to lose a brother, I'm just lucky that I found mine again all these years later. If you ever need someone to talk to, just call me. I feel incredibly lucky getting Callum back although I will have to get used to calling him Jack, but I'm hoping that as well as finding my brother I might have found a sister too? I've always hated being an only child."

She wipes her eyes and smiles through her tears and tells me she is scared of losing Jack.

"Stop talking rubbish." Callum says from the doorway. "Sophie, I know I'm not really your brother but I feel like I am, nothing has changed between us unless you think you might find it tough knowing I'm not actually Jackson."

She shakes her head and hugs him, then puts her arm out to include me and I can feel the prickle of tears in my eyes. Callum breaks away and tells us if anyone should be crying it's him because he's sure that having two sisters in his life won't be easy!

Chris calls up looking for me for me so the three of us walk back down together. I thank Peter and Susan for having us, then I give Carrie a hug and tell her in a mock serious tone to take good care of my niece or nephew. Chris goes out to programme the sat nav but Sophie tells us to ignore it, she says there is a shortcut if we go left and left again there is an old almost unused road that takes us straight onto the main road. It will save us about fifteen minutes.

Susan is hugging her arms tightly around herself and I don't know if it is for warmth or comfort, if I could read her mind I would know she's praying nobody ever discovers what else she did. She is holding a terrible secret.

I say a final goodbye to Callum as I say "See you soon Jack." It feels wrong calling him Jack but that's who he is now, I have to get used to it.

Chapter 34 Lucy

We follow the directions Sophie gave us but we almost miss the partially obscured turning she told us to take, as the car is creeping onto the abandoned road I get the strangest feeling. I shout at Chris to stop the car just as he nears a bend.

"Jesus Lucy, I can't just stop right here." So he moves the car onto the verge looking at me for an explanation,

"I think, well, I feel like I know that this is the tree, the tree that they crashed into. This is where they died, my memories were shattered here that night."

Despite the cold I get out of the car and stand under the bare branches of the tree. I close my eyes and I'm transported back to that night, we are in the campervan, my mum is crying, but not just crying, it's as though she's broken, then I remember that would have been the day we had just lost Callum to the river. My mum is arguing with the man, Wolf. She is telling him we have to stay, Callum might be found, he tells her to stop being so ridiculous and slaps her hard across the face and tells her to stop crying. She's rocking in her seat now calling for Callum, Wolf loses patience with her and reaches across to shake her, she tries to resist him but he is a big man, he grabs her with both of his hands, losing control of the van as he does so and that's when the campervan slams into the tree.

Then there is nothing but silence. A thick empty silence hangs in the air until it is pierced by my screams moments later.

The silence fills my ears as I climb from my little bunk at the back of the van where I have been hiding under my tatty old blankets waiting for Callum to come home, I've been looking through the holes in my blanket, watching my mummy with the nasty man.

The van is all crumpled up at the front and the glass in the windows has shattered and fallen like dust to the ground, I don't understand how my mummy can be asleep, the bang was so loud, she should be awake. I take my blanket and climb out of the space where the window was, I don't want to be near the Wolf man but I need to wait for Callum to come back, and for my mummy to wake up.

I walk along the road a little way but I've forgotten to put my shoes on and the stones are hurting my feet, I don't even know which way to go. There is a patch of grass so I sit down there with my blanket pulled tightly around me, and then as the sun slips out of sight I have a little rest.

"Lucy." Chris is sitting in front of me, we are on the ground. I lean into him and he holds me close as I tell him what I remember. He strokes my hair and listens while I relive those horrifying moments again, I can feel the impact of the crash, my little body being jolted. I know for sure now that my mother really did love Callum and I, she didn't want to give up hope that he would be found. If only she hadn't got into the van with him that night, if she had stayed and kept looking for Callum we might have grown up together as a little family.

I take off my scarf and wrap it around the tree, I tell my mum that I'll bring her some flowers next time I come. Chris takes my hand and leads me back to the car, I feel reluctant to leave but it's so cold out here. I hadn't noticed before but it is starting to snow again, there is a fresh powdery dusting on the ground around me, it's time to move because we've got still got a long journey ahead of us.

Chapter 35 Susan

Nobody can ever know that on the day of the picnic when I was lying next to Peter, listening to the gentle rhythm of his snoring, I heard Jackson and Sophie going off to play their game of hide and seek. They knew they were not allowed to play in the woodland but still I pretended to be asleep and I let them go.

I heard Jackson find Sophie and I opened my eyes and watched her stamp her feet as she got cross at being found so soon. Then I watched Sophie cover her eyes to count while Jackson went off to hide. Then I continued watching as Jackson walked further into the woods, towards the well. I did nothing to stop him. I lay back down and pretended to be asleep. While my little boy fell to his death I did nothing to stop him.

The End

About the author

I live in a small Suffolk town with my husband and two teenage children. I work full time in primary education. In my spare time I read, write, or run. Most of my ideas for stories come to me during an early morning run.

Shattered Memories

Shattered Memories

Shattered Memories

Shattered Memories

Printed in Great Britain
by Amazon